Lightning speared through the sky. Despite the closeness of the atmosphere, Gundersen felt a chill. The drama was reaching its climax. The nildoror were bellowing, stamping, calling to one another with tremendous snorts. They were taking up formations, assembling in aisled rows. Dancing.

Gundersen felt cut off from his own past, even from a sense of his own kinship to his species. All his life he had drawn back from whatever strangeness this planet was offering him. But tonight he felt little allegiance to mankind. He found himself longing to join that black and incomprehensible frenzy at the lakeshore. Something monstrous was running free within him, liberated by the incessant repetition. . . .

He found himself walking down the slope. His feet hesitantly traced out the four-step as he drew near the lake. Did he dare? Would they crush him as blasphemous?

"Yes," the nildoror called to h[illegible] with us!"

And he danced.

DOWNWA[illegible]
by Ro[illegible]g

Author of VALENTINE PONTIFEX and
LORD VALENTINE'S CASTLE

Other Bantam Books by Robert Silverberg
Ask your bookseller for the titles you have missed

THE BOOK OF SKULLS
DOWNWARD TO THE EARTH
LORD VALENTINE'S CASTLE
THE MAJIPOOR CHRONICLES
THE MASKS OF TIME
THORNS
THE WORLD INSIDE

DOWNWARD TO THE EARTH

Robert Silverberg

BANTAM BOOKS
TORONTO · NEW YORK · LONDON · SYDNEY

DOWNWARD TO EARTH

A Bantam Book / published by arrangement with the Author

Bantam edition / February 1984

ISBN 0-553-24043-9

Published simultaneously in the United States and Canada

Bantam Books are published by Bantam Books, Inc. Its trademark, consisting of the words "Bantam Books" and the portrayal of a rooster, is Registered in U.S. Patent and Trademark Office and in other countries. Marca Registrada. Bantam Books, Inc., 666 Fifth Avenue, New York, New York, 10103.

PRINTED IN THE UNITED STATES OF AMERICA

O 0 9 8 7 6 5 4 3 2 1

Who knoweth the spirit of man that goeth upward, and the spirit of the beast that goeth downward to the earth?

ECCLESIASTES 3:21

DOWNWARD TO THE EARTH

One

HE HAD COME back to Holman's World after all. He was not sure why. Call it irresistible attraction; call it sentimentality; call it foolishness. Gundersen had never planned to revisit this place. Yet here he was, waiting for the landing, and there it was in the vision screen, close enough to grasp and squeeze in one hand, a world slightly larger than Earth, a world that had claimed the prime decade of his life, a world where he had learned things about himself that he had not really wanted to know. Now the signal light in the lounge was flashing red. The ship would shortly land. Despite everything, he was coming back.

He saw the shroud of mist that covered the temperate zones, and the great sprawling icecaps, and the girdling blue-black band of the scorched tropics. He remembered riding through the Sea of Dust at blazing twilight, and he remembered a silent, bleak river-journey beneath bowers of twittering dagger-pointed leaves, and he remembered golden cocktails on the veranda of a jungle station on the Night of Five Moons, with Seena close by his side and a herd of nildoror mooing in the bush. That was a long time ago. Now the nildoror were masters of Holman's World again. Gundersen had a hard time accepting that. Perhaps that was the real reason why he had come back: to see what sort of job the nildoror could do.

"Attention, passengers in lounge," came a voice over the

speaker. "We enter landing orbit for Belzagor in fifteen minutes. Please prepare to return to cradles."

Belzagor. That was what they called the planet now. The native name, the nildoror's own word. To Gundersen it seemed like something out of Assyrian mythology. Of course, it was a romanticized pronunciation; coming from a nildor it would really sound more like *Bllls'grr*. Belzagor it was, though. He would try to call the planet by the name it now wore, if that was what he was supposed to do. He attempted never to give needless offense to alien beings.

"Belzagor," he said. "It's a voluptuous sound, isn't it? Rolls nicely off the tongue."

The tourist couple beside him in the ship's lounge nodded. They agreed readily with whatever Gundersen said. The husband, plump, pale, overdressed, said, "They were still calling it Holman's World when you were last out here, weren't they?"

"Oh, yes," Gundersen said. "But that was back in the good old imperialist days, when an Earthman could call a planet whatever he damn pleased. That's all over now."

The tourist wife's lips tightened in that thin, pinched, dysmenorrheal way of hers. Gundersen drew a somber pleasure from annoying her. All during the voyage he had deliberately played a role out of Kipling for these tourists—posing as the former colonial administrator going out to see what a beastly botch the natives must be making out of the task of governing themselves. It was an exaggeration, a distortion, of his real attitude, but sometimes it pleased him to wear masks. The tourists—there were eight of them—looked upon him in mingled awe and contempt as he swaggered among them, a big fair-skinned man with the mark of outworld experience stamped on his features. They disapproved of him, of the image of himself that he gave them; and yet they knew he had suffered and labored and striven under a foreign sun, and there was romance in that.

"Will you be staying at the hotel?" the tourist husband asked.

"Oh, no. I'm going right out into the bush, toward the mist country. Look—there, you see? In the northern hemisphere, that band of clouds midway up. The temperature gradient's very steep: tropic and arctic practically side by side. Mist. Fog. They'll take you on a tour of it. I have some business in there."

"Business? I thought these new independent worlds were outside the zone of economic penetration that—"

"Not commercial business," Gundersen said. "Personal business. Unfinished business. Something I didn't manage to discover during my tour of duty here." The signal light flashed again, more insistently. "Will you excuse me? We really should cradle up now."

He went to his cabin and readied himself for landing. Webfoam spurted from the spinnerets and enfolded him. He closed his eyes. He felt deceleration thrust, that curiously archaic sensation hearkening back to space travel's earliest days. The ship dropped planetward as Gundersen swayed, suspended, insulated from the worst of the velocity change.

Belzagor's only spaceport was the one that Earthmen had built more than a hundred years before. It was in the tropics, at the mouth of the great river flowing into Belzagor's single ocean. Madden's River, Benjamini Ocean—Gundersen didn't know the nildoror names at all. The spaceport was self-maintaining, fortunately. Automatic high-redundancy devices operated the landing beacon; homeostatic surveillance kept the pad repaved and the bordering jungle cropped back. All, all by machine; it was unrealistic to expect the nildoror to operate a spaceport, and impossible to keep a crew of Earthmen stationed here to do it. Gundersen understood that there were still perhaps a hundred Earthmen living on Belzagor, even after the general withdrawal, but they were not such as would operate a spaceport. And there was a treaty, in any case. Administrative functions were to be performed by nildoror, or not at all.

They landed. The webfoam cradle dissolved upon signal. They went out of the ship.

The air had the tropical reek: rich loam, rotting leaves, the droppings of jungle beasts, the aroma of creamy flowers. It was early evening. A couple of the moons were out. As always, the threat of rain was in the air; the humidity was 99%, probably. But that threat almost never materialized. Rainstorms were rare in this tropical belt. The water simply precipitated out of the air in droplets all the time, imperceptibly coating you with fine wet beads. Gundersen saw lightning flicker beyond the tops of the hullygully trees at the edge of the pad. A stewardess marshaled the nine debarkees. "This way, please," she said crisply, and led them toward the one building.

On the left, three nildoror emerged from the bush and solemnly gazed at the newcomers. Tourists gasped and pointed. "Look! Do you see them? Like elephants, they are! Are those nili—nildoror?"

"Nildoror, yes," Gundersen said. The tang of the big beasts drifted across the clearing. A bull and two cows, he guessed, judging by the size of the tusks. They were all about the same height, three meters plus, with the deep green skins that marked them as western-hemisphere nildoror. Eyes as big as platters peered back at him in dim curiosity. The short-tusked cow in front lifted her tail and placidly dropped an avalanche of steaming purple dung. Gundersen heard deep blurred sounds, but at this distance he could not make out what the nildoror were saying. Imagine them running a spaceport, he thought. Imagine them running a planet. But they do. But they do.

There was no one in the spaceport building. Some robots, part of the homeostasis net, were repairing the wall at the far side, where the gray plastic sheeting had apparently succumbed to spore implantation; sooner or later the jungle rot got everything in this part of the planet. But that was the only visible activity. There was no customs desk. The nildoror did not have a bureaucracy of that sort. They did not care what you brought with you to their world. The nine passengers had undergone a customs inspection on Earth, just before setting out; Earth did care, very much, what was taken to undeveloped planets. There was also no spaceline office here, nor were there money-changing booths, nor newsstands, nor any of the other concessions one normally finds in a spaceport. There was only a big bare shed, which once had been the nexus of a bustling colonial outpost, in the days when Holman's World had been the property of Earth. It seemed to Gundersen that he saw ghosts of those days all about him: figures in tropical khaki carrying messages, supercargoes waving inventory sheets, computer technicians draped in festoons of memory beads, nildoror bearers laden with outgoing produce. Now all was still. The scrapings of the repair robots echoed across the emptiness.

The spaceline stewardess was telling the eight passengers, "Your guide should be here any minute. He'll take you to the hotel, and—"

Gundersen was supposed to go to the hotel too, just for tonight. In the morning he hoped to arrange for transport. He had no formal plans for his northward journey; it was going to be largely an improvisation, a reconnaissance into his own pockmarked past.

He said to the stewardess, "Is the guide a nildor?"

"You mean, native? Oh, no, he's an Earthman, Mr. Gundersen." She rummaged in a sheaf of printout slips. "His name's Van Beneker, and he was supposed to be here at least half an hour before the ship landed, so I don't understand why—"

"Van Beneker was never strong on punctuality," Gundersen said. "But there he is."

A beetle, much rusted and stained by the climate, had pulled up at the open entrance to the building, and from it now was coming a short red-haired man, also much rusted and stained by the climate. He wore rumpled fatigues and a pair of knee-high jungle boots. His hair was thinning and his tanned bald skull showed through the slicked-down strands. He entered the building and peered around, blinking. His eyes were light blue and faintly hyperthyroid-looking.

"Van?" Gundersen said. "Over here, Van."

The little man came over. In a hurried, perfunctory way he said, while he was still far from them, "I want to welcome all you people to Belzagor, as Holman's World is now known. My name's Van Beneker, and I'm going to show you as much of this fascinating planet as is legally permissible to show you, and—"

"Hello, Van," Gundersen cut in.

The guide halted, obviously irritated, in mid-spiel. He blinked again and looked closely at Gundersen. Finally he said, clearly not believing it, "Mr. Gundersen?"

"Just Gundersen. I'm not your boss any more."

"Jesus, Mr. Gundersen. Jesus, are you here for the tour?"

"Not exactly, I'm here to take my own tour."

Van Beneker said to the others, "I want you to excuse me. Just for a minute." To the spaceline stewardess he said, "It's okay. You can officially convey them to me. I take responsibility. They are all here? One, two, three—eight. That's right. Okay, the luggage goes out there, next to the beetle. Tell them all to wait. I'll be right with them." He tugged at Gundersen's elbow. "Come on over here, Mr. Gundersen. You don't know how amazed I am. Jesus!"

"How have you been, Van?"

"Lousy. How else, on this planet? When did you leave, exactly?"

"2240. The year after relinquishment. Eight years ago."

"Eight years. And what have you been doing?"

"The home office found work for me." Gundersen said. "I keep busy. Now I've got a year's accumulated leave."

"To spend it *here*?"

"Why not?"

"What for?"

"I'm going up mist country," Gundersen said. "I want to visit the sulidoror."

"You don't want to do that," said Van Beneker. "What do you want to do that for?"

"To satisfy a curiosity."

"There's only trouble when a man goes up there. You know the stories, Mr. Gundersen. I don't need to remind you, how many guys went up there, how many didn't come back." Van Beneker laughed. "You didn't come all the way to this place just to rub noses with the sulidoror. I bet you got some other reason."

Gundersen let the point pass. "What do you do here now, Van?"

"Tourist guide, mostly. We get nine, ten batches a year. I take them up along the ocean, then show them a bit of the mist country, then we hop across the Sea of Dust. It's a nice little tour."

"Yes."

"The rest of the time I relax. I talk to the nildoror a lot, and sometimes I visit friends at the bush stations. You'll know everyone, Mr. Gundersen. It's all the old people, still out there."

"What about Seena Royce?" Gundersen asked.

"She's up by Shangri-la Falls."

"Still have her looks?"

"She thinks so," Van Beneker said. "You figure you'll go up that way?"

"Of course," Gundersen said. "I'm making a sentimental pilgrimage. I'll tour all the bush stations. See the old friends. Seena. Cullen. Kurtz. Salamone. Whoever's still there."

"Some of them are dead."

"Whoever's still there," Gundersen said. He looked down at the little man and smiled. "You'd better take care of your tourists, now. We can talk at the hotel tonight. I want you to fill me in on everything that's happened while I've been gone."

"Easy, Mr. Gundersen. I can do it right now in one word. Rot. Everything's rotting. Look at the spaceport wall over there."

"I see."

"Look at the repair robots, now. They don't shine much, do they? They're giving out too. If you get close, you can see the spots on their hulls."

"But homeostasis—"

"Sure. Everything gets repaired, even the repair robots. But the system's going to break down. Sooner or later, the rot will get into the basic programs, and then there won't be any more repairs, and this world will go straight back into the stone age. I mean *all* the way back. And then the nildoror will finally be happy. I understand those big bastards as much as anybody does. I know they can't wait to see the last trace of Earthmen rot right off this planet. They pretend they're friendly, but the hate's there all the time, real sick hate, and—"

"You ought to look after your tourists, Van," Gundersen said. "They're getting restless."

Two

A CARAVAN OF nildoror was going to transport them from the spaceport to the hotel—two Earthmen per alien, with Gundersen riding alone, and Van Beneker, with the luggage, leading the way in his beetle. The three nildoror grazing at the edge of the field ambled over to enroll in the caravan, and two others emerged from the bush. Gundersen was surprised that nildoror were still willing to act as beasts of burden for Earthmen. 'They don't mind,'' Van Beneker explained. ''They like to do us favors. It makes them feel superior. They can't hardly tell there's weight on them, anyhow. And they don't think there's anything shameful about letting people ride them.''

''When I was here I had the impression they resented it,'' Gundersen said.

''Since relinquishment they take things like that easier. Anyway, how could you be sure what they thought? I mean, what they *really* thought.''

The tourists were a little alarmed at riding nildoror. Van Beneker tried to calm them by telling them it was an important part of the Belzagor experience. Besides, he added, machinery did not thrive on this planet and there were hardly any functioning beetles left. Gundersen demonstrated how to mount, for the benefit of the apprehensive newcomers. He tapped his nildor's left-hand tusk, and the alien knelt in its elephantine way, ponderously coming down on its front knees, then its back ones. The nildor wriggled its shoulders, in effect dislocating them to create the deep swayback valley in which a man could ride so comfortably, and Gundersen climbed aboard, seizing the short backward-thrusting horns as his pommels. The spiny crest down the middle of the alien's broad skull began to twitch. Gundersen recognized it as a gesture of welcome; the nildoror had a rich language of gesture, employing not only the spines but also their long ropy trunks and their many-pleated ears. "*Sssukh!*" Gundersen said, and the nildor arose. "Do you sit well?" it asked him in its own language. "Very well indeed," Gundersen said, feeling a surge of delight as the unforgotten vocabulary came to his lips.

In their clumsy, hesitant way, the eight tourists did as he had done, and the caravan set out down the river road toward the hotel. Nightflies cast a dim glow under the canopy of trees. A third moon was in the sky, and the mingled lights came through the leaves, revealing the oily, fast-moving river just to their left. Gundersen stationed himself at the rear of the procession in case one of the tourists had a mishap. There was only one uneasy moment, though, when a nildor paused and left the rank. It rammed the triple prongs of its tusks into the riverbank to grub up some morsel, and then resumed its place in line. In the old days, Gundersen knew, that would never have happened. Nildoror were not permitted then to have whims.

He enjoyed the ride. The jouncing strides were agreeable, and the pace was swift without being strenuous for the passengers. What good beasts these nildoror are, Gundersen thought. Strong, docile, intelligent. He almost reached forward to stroke his mount's spines, deciding at the last moment that it would seem patronizing. The nildoror are something other than funny-looking elephants, he reminded himself. They are intelligent beings, the dominant life forms of their planet, *people,* and don't you forget it.

Soon Gundersen could hear the crashing of the surf. They were nearing the hotel.

The path widened to become a clearing. Up ahead, one of the tourist women pointed into the bush; her husband shrugged and shook his head. When Gundersen reached that place he saw what was bothering them. Black shapes crouched between the trees, and dark figures were moving slowly to and fro. They were barely visible in the shadows. As Gundersen's nildor went past, two of the dim forms emerged and stood by the edge of the path. They were husky bipeds, close to three meters tall, covered with thick coats of dark red hair. Massive tails swished slowly through the greenish gloom. Hooded eyes, slit-wide even in this scant light, appraised the procession. Drooping rubbery snouts, tapir-long, sniffed audibly.

A woman turned gingerly and said to Gundersen, "What are they?"

"Sulidoror. The secondary species. They come from up mist country. These are northern ones."

"Are they dangerous?"

"I wouldn't call them that."

"If they're northern animals, why are they down here?" her husband wanted to know.

"I'm not sure," Gundersen said. He questioned his mount and received an answer. "They work at the hotel," Gundersen called ahead. "Bellhops. Kitchen hands." It seemed strange to him that the nildoror would have turned the sulidoror into domestic servants at an Earthman's hotel. Not even before relinquishment had sulidoror been used as servants. But of course there had been plenty of robots here then.

The hotel lay just ahead. It was on the coast, a glistening geodesic dome that showed no external signs of decay. Before relinquishment, it had been a posh resort run exclusively for the benefit of the top-level administrators of the Company. Gundersen had spent many happy hours in it. Now he dismounted, and he and Van Beneker helped the tourists down. Three sulidoror stood at the hotel entrance. Van Beneker gestured fiercely at them and they began to take the luggage from the beetle's storage hold.

Inside, Gundersen quickly detected symptoms of decline. A carpet of tiger-moss had begun to edge out of an ornamental garden strip along the lobby wall, and was starting to reach onto the fine black slabs of the main hall's floor; he saw the toothy little mouths hopefully snapping as he walked in. No doubt the hotel's maintenance robots once had been programmed to cut the ornamental moss back to the border of the garden bed, but the program must have subtly altered with the years so that now the moss was allowed to intrude on the interior of the building as well. Possibly the robots were gone altogether, and the sulidoror who had replaced them were lax in their pruning duties. And there were other hints that control was slipping away.

"The boys will show you to your rooms," Van Beneker said. "You can come down for cocktails whenever you're ready. Dinner will be served in about an hour and a half."

A towering sulidor conducted Gundersen to a third-floor room overlooking the sea. Reflex led him to offer the huge creature a coin; but the sulidor merely looked blankly at him and did not venture to take it. It seemed to Gundersen that there was a suppressed tension about the sulidor, an inward seething, but perhaps it existed only in his own imagination. In the old days sulidoror had rarely been seen outside the zone of mist, and Gundersen did not feel at ease with them.

In nildoror words he said, "How long have you been at the hotel?" But the sulidor did not respond. Gundersen did not know the language of the sulidoror, but he was aware that every sulidor was supposed to speak fluent nildororu as well as sulidororu. Enunciating more clearly, he repeated his question. The sulidor scratched its pelt with gleaming claws and said nothing. Moving past Gundersen, it deopaqued the window-wall, adjusted the atmospheric filters, and stalked solemnly out.

Gundersen frowned. Quickly he stripped and got under the cleanser. A quick whirr of vibration took from him the grime of his day's journey. He unpacked and donned evening clothes, a close gray tunic, polished boots, a mirror for his brow. He toned the color of his hair down the spectrum a short distance, dimming it from yellow almost to auburn.

Suddenly he felt very tired.

He was just into early middle years, only forty-eight, and travel ordinarily did not affect him. Why this fatigue, then? He realized that he had been holding himself unusually stiff these few hours he had been back on this planet. Rigid, inflexible, tense—uncertain of his motives in returning, unsure of his welcome, perhaps touched a bit by curdled guilts, and now the strain was telling. He touched a switch and made the wall a mirror. Yes, his face was drawn; the cheekbones, always prominent, now jutted like blades, and the lips were clamped and the forehead was furrowed. The thin slab of his nose was distended by tension-flared nostrils. Gundersen shut his eyes and went through one of the drills of a relaxation mode. He looked better thirty seconds later; but a drink might help, he decided. He went down to the lounge.

None of the tourists were there yet. The louvers were open, and he heard the roar and crash of the sea, smelled its saltiness. A white curdled line of accumulated salt had been allowed to form along the margin of the beach. The tide was in; only the tips of the jagged rocks that framed the bathing area were visible. Gundersen looked out over the moonslight-streaked water, staring into the blackness of the eastern horizon. Three moons had also been up on his last night here, when they gave the farewell party for him. And after the revelry was over, he and Seena had gone for a midnight swim, out to the tide-hidden shoal where they could barely stand, and when they returned to shore, naked and salt-encrusted, he had made love to her behind the rocks, embracing her for what he was sure would be the last time. And now he was back.

He felt a stab of nostalgia so powerful that he winced.

Gundersen had been thirty years old when he came out to Holman's World as an assistant station agent. He had been forty, and a sector administrator, when he left. In a sense the first thirty years of his life had been a pale prelude to that decade, and the last eight years of it had been a hollow epilogue. He had lived his life on this silent continent, bounded by mist and ice to the north, mist and ice to the south, the Benjamini Ocean to the east, the Sea of Dust to the west. For a while he had ruled half a world, at least in the absence of the chief resident; and this planet had shrugged him off as though he had never been. Gundersen turned away from the louvers and sat down.

Van Beneker appeared, still in his sweaty, rumpled fatigues. He winked cordially at Gundersen and began rummaging in a cabinet. "I'm the bartender too, Mr. G. What can

I get you?"

"Alcohol," Gundersen said. "Any form you recommend."

"Snout or flask?"

"Flask. I like the taste."

"As you say. But snout for me. It's the effect, sir, the *effect.*" He set an empty glass before Gundersen and handed him a flask containing three ounces of a dark red fluid. Highland rum, local product. Gundersen hadn't tasted it in eight years. The flask was equipped with its own condensation chiller; Gundersen thumbed it with a quick short push and quietly watched the flakes of ice beginning to form along the inside. When his drink was properly chilled he poured it and put it quickly to his lips.

"That's pre-relinquishment stock," Van Beneker said. "Not much of it left, but I knew you'd appreciate it." He was holding an ultrasonic tube to his left forearm. *Zzz!* and the snout spurted alcohol straight into his vein. Van Beneker grinned. "Works faster this way. The working-class man's boozer. Eh? Eh? Get you another rum, Mr. G?"

"Not just yet. Better look after your tourists, Van."

The tourist couples were beginning to enter the bar: first the Watsons, then the Mirafloreses, the Steins, finally the Christophers. Evidently they had expected to find the bar throbbing with life, full of other tourists giddily hailing one another from distant parts of the room, and red-jacketed waiters ferrying drinks. Instead there were peeling plastic walls, a sonic sculpture that no longer worked and was deeply cobwebbed, empty tables, and that unpleasant Mr. Gundersen moodily peering into a glass. The tourists exchanged cheated glances. Was this what they had spanned the light-years to see? Van Beneker went to them, offering drinks, weeds, whatever else the limited resources of the hotel might be able to supply. They settled in two groups near the windows and began to talk in low voices, plainly self-conscious in front of Gundersen. Surely they felt the foolishness of their roles, these soft well-to-do people whose boredom had driven them to peer at the remote reaches of the galaxy. Stein ran a helix parlor in California, Miraflores a chain of lunar casinos, Watson was a doctor, and Christopher—Gundersen could not remember what Christopher did. Something in the financial world.

Mrs. Stein said, "There are some of those animals on the beach. The green elephants."

Everyone looked. Gundersen signaled for another drink, and got it. Van Beneker, flushed, sweating, winked again and put a second snout to his arm. The tourists began to titter. Mrs. Christopher said, "Don't they have any shame at all?"

"Maybe they're simply playing, Ethel," Watson said.

"*Playing?* Well, if you call that playing—"

Gundersen leaned forward, glancing out the window without getting up. On the beach a pair of nildoror were coupling, the cow kneeling where the salt was thickest, the bull mounting her, gripping her shoulders, pressing his central tusk down firmly against the spiny crest of her skull, jockeying his hindquarters about as he made ready for the consummating thrust. The tourists, giggling, making heavy-handed comments of appreciation, seemed both shocked and titillated. To his considerable surprise, Gundersen realized he was shocked, too, although coupling nildoror were nothing new to him; and when a ferocious orgasmic bellowing rose from below he glanced away, embarrassed and not understanding why.

"You look upset," Van Beneker said.

"They didn't have to do that *here*."

"Why not? They do it all over the place. You know how it is."

"They deliberately went out there," Gundersen muttered. "To show off for the tourists? Or to annoy the tourists? They shouldn't be reacting to the tourists at all. What are they trying to prove? That they're just animals, I suppose."

"You don't understand the nildoror, Gundy."

Gundersen looked up, startled as much by Van Beneker's words as by the sudden descent from "Mr. Gundersen" to "Gundy." Van Beneker seemed startled, too, blinking rapidly and tugging at a stray sparse lock of fading hair.

"I don't?" Gundersen asked. "After spending ten years here?"

"Begging pardon, but I never did think you understood them, even when you were here. I used to go around with you a lot to the villages when I was clerking for you. I watched you."

"In what way do you think I failed to understand them, Van?"

"You despised them. You thought of them as animals."

"That isn't so!"

"Sure it is, Gundy. You never once admitted they had any intelligence at all."

"That's absolutely untrue," Gundersen said. He got up and took a new flask of rum from the cabinet, and returned to the table.

"I would have gotten that for you," Van Beneker said. "You just had to ask me."

"It's all right." Gundersen chilled the drink and downed it fast. "You're talking a load of nonsense, Van. I did everything possible for those people. To improve them, to lift them toward civilization. I requisitioned tapes for them, sound pods, culture by the ton. I put through new regulations about maximum labor. I insisted that my men respect their rights as the dominant indigenous culture. I—"

"You treated them like very intelligent animals. Not like intelligent alien *people*. Maybe you didn't even realize it yourself, Gundy, but I did, and God knows they did. You talked down to them. You were kind to them in the wrong way. All your interest in uplifting them, in improving them—crap, Gundy, they have their own culture. They didn't want yours!"

"It was my duty to guide them," Gundersen said stiffly. "Futile though it was to think that a bunch of animals who don't have a written language, who don't—" He stopped, horrified.

"Animals," Van Beneker said.

"I'm tired. Maybe I've had too much to drink. It just slipped out."

"Animals."

"Stop pushing me, Van. I did the best I could, and if what I was doing was wrong, I'm sorry. I tried to do what was right." Gundersen pushed his empty glass forward. "Get me another, will you?"

Van Beneker fetched the drink, and one more snout for

himself. Gundersen welcomed the break in the conversation, and apparently Van Beneker did, too, for they both remained silent a long moment, avoiding each other's eyes. A sulidor entered the bar and began to gather the empties, crouching to keep from grazing the Earthman-scaled ceiling. The chatter of the tourists died away as the fierce-looking creature moved through the room. Gundersen looked toward the beach. The nildoror were gone. One of the moons was setting in the east, leaving a fiery track across the surging water. He realized that he had forgotten the names of the moons. No matter; the old Earthman-given names were dead history now. He said finally to Van Beneker, "How come you decided to stay here after relinquishment?"

"I felt at home here. I've been here twenty-five years. Why should I go anywhere else?"

"No family ties elsewhere?"

"No. And it's comfortable here. I get a company pension. I get tips from the tourists. There's a salary from the hotel. That's enough to keep me supplied with what I need. What I need, mostly, is snouts. Why should I leave?"

"Who owns the hotel?" Gundersen asked.

"The confederation of western-continent nildoror. The Company gave it to them."

"And the nildoror pay you a salary? I thought they were outside the galactic money economy."

"They are. They arranged something with the Company."

"What you're saying is the Company still runs this hotel."

"If anybody can be said to run it, the Company does, yes," Van Beneker agreed. "But that isn't much of a violation of the relinquishment law. There's only one employee. Me. I pocket my salary from what the tourists pay for accommodations. The rest I spend on imports from the money sphere. Don't you see, Gundy, it's all just a big joke? It's a routine designed to allow me to bring in liquor, that's all. This hotel isn't a commercial proposition. The Company is really out of this planet. Completely."

"All right. All right. I believe you."

Van Beneker said, "What are you looking for up mist country?"

"You really want to know?"

"It passes the time to ask things."

"I want to watch the rebirth ceremony. I never saw it, all the time I was here."

The bulging blue eyes seemed to bulge even more. "Why can't you be serious, Gundy?"

"I am."

"It's dangerous to fool with the rebirth thing."

"I'm prepared for the risks."

"You ought to talk to some people here about it, first. It's not a thing for us to meddle in."

Gundersen sighed. "Have you seen it?"

"No. Never. Never even been interested in seeing it. Whatever the hell the sulidoror do in the mountains, let them do it without me. I'll tell you who to talk to, though. Seena."

"She's watched the rebirth?"

"Her husband has."

Gundersen felt a spasm of dismay. "Who's her husband?"

"Jeff Kurtz. You didn't know?"

"I'll be damned," Gundersen murmured.

"You wonder what she saw in him, eh?"

"I wonder that she could bring herself to live with a man like that. You talk about *my* attitude toward the natives! There's someone who treated them like his own property, and—"

"Talk to Seena, up at Shangri-la Falls. About the rebirth." Van Beneker laughed. "You're playing games with me, aren't you? You know I'm drunk and you're having a little fun."

"No. Not at all." Gundersen rose uneasily. "I ought to get some sleep now."

Van Beneker followed him to the door. Just as Gundersen went out, the little man leaned close to him and said, "You know, Gundy, what the nildoror were doing on the beach before—they weren't doing that for the tourists. They were doing it for you. It's the kind of sense of humor they have. Good night, Gundy."

Three

GUNDERSEN WOKE EARLY. His head was surprisingly clear. It was just a little after dawn, and the green-tinged sun was low in the sky. The eastern sky, out over the ocean: a welcome touch of Earthliness. He went down to the beach for a swim. A soft south wind was blowing, pushing a few clouds into view. The hullygully trees were heavy with fruit; the humidity was as high as ever; thunder boomed back from the mountains that ran in an arc paralleling the coast a day's drive inland. Mounds of nildoror dung were all over the beach. Gundersen stepped warily, zigzagging over the crunching sand and hurling himself flat into the surf. He went under the first curling row of breakers and with quick powerful strokes headed toward the shoals. The tide was low. He crossed the exposed sandbar and swam beyond it until he felt himself tiring. When he returned to the shore area, he found two of the tourist men had also come out for a swim, Christopher and Miraflores. They smiled tentatively at him. ''Bracing,'' he said. ''Nothing like salt water.''

''Why can't they keep the beach clean, though?'' Miraflores asked.

A sullen sulidor served breakfast. Native fruits, native fish. Gundersen's appetite was immense. He bolted down three golden-green bitterfruits for a start, then expertly boned a whole spiderfish and forked the sweet pink flesh into himself as though engaged in a speed contest. The sulidor brought him another fish and a bowl of phallic-looking forest candles. Gundersen still was working on these when Van Beneker entered, wearing clean though frayed clothes. He looked bloodshot and chastened. Instead of joining Gundersen at the table he merely smiled a perfunctory greeting and sailed past.

"Sit with me, Van," Gundersen said.

Uncomfortably, Van Beneker complied. "About last night—"

"Forget it."

"I was insufferable, Mr. Gundersen."

"You were in your cups. Forgiven. In vino veritas. You were calling me Gundy last night, too. You may as well do it this morning. Who catches the fish?"

"There's an automatic weir just north of the hotel. Catches them and pipes them right into the kitchen. God knows who'd prepare food here if we didn't have the machines."

"And who picks the fruit? Machines?"

"The sulidoror do that," Van Beneker said.

"When did sulidoror start working as menials on this planet?"

"About five years ago. Six, maybe. The nildoror got the idea from us, I suppose. If we could turn them into bearers and living bulldozers, they could turn the sulidoror into bellhops. After all, the sulidoror *are* the inferior species."

"But always their own masters. Why did they agree to serve? What's in it for them?"

"I don't know," Van Beneker said. "When did anybody ever understand the sulidoror?"

True enough, Gundersen thought. No one yet had succeeded in making sense out of the relationship between this planet's two intelligent species. The presence of two intelligent species, in the first place, went against the general evolutionary logic of the universe. Both nildoror and sulidoror qualified for autonomous ranking, with perception levels beyond those of the higher hominoid primates; a sulidor was considerably smarter than a chimpanzee, and a nildor was a good deal more clever than that. If there had been no nildoror here at all, the presence of the sulidoror alone would have been enough to force the Company to relinquish possession of the planet when the decolonization movement reached its peak. But why two species, and why the strange unspoken accommodation between them, the bipedal carnivorous sulidoror ruling over the mist country, the quadrupedal herbivorous nildoror dominating the tropics? How had they carved this world up so neatly? And why was the division of authority breaking down, if breaking down was really what was happening? Gundersen knew that there were ancient treaties between these creatures, that a system of claims and prerogatives existed, that every nildor went back to the mist country when the time for its rebirth arrived. But he did not know what role the sulidoror really played in the life and the rebirth of the nildoror. No one did. The pull of that mystery was, he admitted, one of the things that had brought him back to Holman's World, to Belzagor, now that he had shed his administrative responsibilities and was free to risk his life indulging private curiosities. The shift in the nildoror-sulidoror relationship that seemed to be taking place around this hotel troubled him, though; it had been hard enough to comprehend that relationship when it was static. Of course, the habits of alien beings were none of his business, really. Nothing was his business, these days. When a man had no business, he had to appoint himself to some. So he was here to do research, ostensibly, which is to say to snoop and spy. Putting it that way made his return to this planet seem more like an act of will, and less like the yielding to irresistible compulsion that he feared it had been.

"—more complicated than anybody ever thought," Van Beneker was saying.

"I'm sorry. I must have missed most of what you said."

"It isn't important. We theorize a lot, here. The last hundred of us. How soon do you start north?"

"In a hurry to be rid of me, Van?"

"Only trying to make plans, sir," the little man said, hurt. "If you're staying, we need provisions for you, and—"

"I'm leaving after breakfast. If you'll tell me how to get to the nearest nildoror encampment so I can apply for my travel permit."

"Twenty kilometers, southeast. I'd run you down there in the beetle, but you understand—the tourists—"

"Can you get me a ride with a nildor?" Gundersen suggested. "If it's too much bother, I suppose I can hike it, but—"

"I'll arrange things," Van Beneker said.

A young male nildor appeared an hour after breakfast to take Gundersen down to the encampment. In the old days Gundersen would simply have climbed on his back, but now he felt the necessity of making introductions. One does not ask an autonomous intelligent being to carry you twenty kilometers through the jungle, he thought, without attempting to enter into elementary courtesies. "I am Edmund Gundersen of the first birth," he said, "and I wish you joy of many rebirths, friend of my journey."

"I am Srin'gahar of the first birth," replied the nildor evenly, "and I thank you for your wish, friend of my journey. I serve you of free choice and await your commands."

"I must speak with a many-born one and gain permission to travel north. The man here says you will take me to such a one."

"So it can be done. Now?"

"Now."

Gundersen had one suitcase. He rested it on the nildor's broad rump and Srin'gahar instantly curved his tail up and back to clamp the bag in place. Then the nildor knelt and Gundersen went through the ritual of mounting. Tons of powerful flesh rose and moved obediently toward the rim of the forest. It was almost as though nothing had ever changed.

They traveled the first kilometer in silence, through an ever-thickening series of bitterfruit glades. Gradually it occurred to Gundersen that the nildor was not going to speak unless spoken to, and he opened the conversation by remarking that he had lived for ten years on Belzagor. Srin'gahar said that he knew that; he remembered Gundersen from the era of Company rule. The nature of the nildoror vocal system drained overtones and implications from the statement. It came out flat, a mooing nasal grunt that did not reveal whether the nildor remembered Gundersen fondly, bitterly, or indifferently. Gundersen might have drawn a hint from the movements of Srin'gahar's cranial crest, but it was impossible for someone seated on a nildor's back to detect any but the broadest movements. The intricate nildoror system of non-verbal supplementary communication had not evolved for the convenience of passengers. In any event Gundersen had known only a few of the almost infinite number of supplementary gestures, and he had forgotten most of those. But the nildor seemed courteous enough.

Gundersen took advantage of the ride to practice his nildororu. So far he had done well, but in an interview with a many-born one he would need all the verbal skill he could muster. Again and again he said, "I spoke that the right way, didn't I? Correct me if I didn't."

"You speak very well," Srin'gahar insisted.

Actually the language was not difficult. It was narrow in range, simple in grammar. Nildororu words did not inflect; they agglutinated, piling syllable atop syllable so that a complex concept like "the former grazing-ground of my mate's clan" emerged as a long grumbled growl of sound unbroken even by a brief pause. Nildoror speech was slow and stolid, requiring broad rolling tones that an Earthman had to launch from the roots of his nostrils; when Gundersen shifted from nildororu to any Earth language, he felt sudden exhilaration, like a circus acrobat transported instantaneously from Jupiter to Mercury.

Srin'gahar was taking a nildoror path, not one of the old Company roads. Gundersen had to duck low-hanging branches now and then, and once a quivering nicalanga vine descended to catch him around the throat in a gentle, cool, quickly broken, and yet frightening embrace. When he looked back, he saw the vine tumescent with excitement, red and swollen from the thrill of caressing an Earthman's skin. Shortly the jungle humidity reached the top of the scale and the level of condensation became something close to that of rain; the air was so wet that Gundersen had trouble breathing, and streams of sweat poured down his body. The sticky moment passed. Minutes later they intersected a Company road. It was a narrow fading track in the jungle, nearly overgrown. In another year it would be gone.

The nildor's vast body demanded frequent feedings. Every half hour they halted and Gundersen dismounted while Srin'gahar munched shrubbery. The sight fed Gundersen's latent prejudices, troubling him so much that he tried not to look. In a wholly elephantine way the nildor uncoiled his trunk and ripped leafy branches from low trees; then the great mouth sagged open and in the bundle went. With his triple tusks Srin'gahar shredded slabs of bark for dessert. The big jaws moved back and forth tirelessly, grinding, milling. We are no prettier when we eat, Gundersen told himself, and the demon within him counterpointed his tolerance with a shrill insistence that his companion was a beast.

Srin'gahar was not an outgoing type. When Gundersen said nothing, the nildor said nothing; when Gundersen asked a question, the nildor replied politely but minimally. The strain of sustaining such a broken-backed conversation drained Gundersen, and he allowed long minutes to pass in silence. Caught up in the rhythm of the big creature's steady stride, he was content to be carried effortlessly along through the steamy jungle. He had no idea where he was and could not even tell if they were going in the right direction, for the trees far overhead met in a closed canopy, screening the sun. After the nildor had stopped for his third meal of the morning, though, he gave Gunderson an unexpected clue to their location. Cutting away from the path in a sudden diagonal, the nildor trotted a short distance into the most dense part of the forest, battering down the vegetation, and came to a halt in front of what once had been a Company building—a glassy dome now dimmed by time and swathed in vines.

"Do you know this house, Edmund of the first birth?" Srin'gahar asked.

"What was it?"

"The serpent station. Where you gathered the juices."

The past abruptly loomed like a toppling cliff above Gundersen. Jagged hallucinatory images plucked at his mind. Ancient scandals, long forgotten or suppressed, sprang to new life. This is the serpent station, this ruin? This the place of private sins, the scene of so many falls from grace? Gundersen felt his cheeks reddening. He slipped from the nildor's back and walked haltingly toward the building. He stood at the door a moment, looking in. Yes, there were the hanging tubes and pipes, the runnels through which the extracted venom had flowed, all the processing equipment still in place, half devoured by warmth and moisture and neglect. There was the entrance for the jungle serpents, drawn by alien music they could not resist, and there they were milked of their venom and there—and there—

Gundersen glanced back at Srin'gahar. The spines of the nildor's crest were distended: a mark of tension, a mark perhaps of shared shame. The nildoror, too, had memories of this building. Gundersen stepped into the station, pushing back the half-open door. It split loose from its moorings as he did so, and a musical tremor ran *whang whang whang* through the whole of the spherical building, dying away to a blurred feeble tinkle. *Whang* and Gundersen heard Jeff Kurtz's guitar again, and the years fell away and he was thirty-one years old once more, a newcomer on Holman's World and about to begin his first stint at the serpent station, finally assigned to that place that was the focus of so much gossip. Yes. Out of the shroud of memory came the image of Kurtz. There he was standing just inside the station door, impossibly tall, the tallest man Gundersen had ever seen, with a great pale domed hairless head and enormous dark eyes socketed in prehistoric-looking bony ridges, and a bright-toothed smile that ran at least a kilometer's span from cheek to cheek. The guitar went *whang* and Kurtz said, "You'll find it interesting here, Gundy. This station is a unique experience. We buried your predecessor last week." *Whang*. "Of course, you must learn to establish a distance between yourself and what happens here. That's the secret of maintaining your identity on an alien world, Gundy. Comprehend the esthetics of distance: draw a boundary line about yourself and say to the planet, thus far you can go in consuming me, and no farther. Otherwise the planet will eventually absorb you and make you part of it. Am I being clear?"

"Not at all," said Gundersen.

"The meaning will manifest itself eventually." *Whang*. "Come see our serpents."

Kurtz was five years older than Gundersen and had been on Holman's World three years longer. Gundersen had known him by reputation long before meeting him. Everyone seemed to feel awe of Kurtz, and yet he was only an assistant station agent, who had never been promoted beyond that lowly rank. After five minutes of exposure to him, Gundersen thought he knew why. Kurtz gave an impression of instability—not quite a fallen angel but certainly a falling one, Lucifer on his way down, descending from morn to noon, noon to dewy eve, but now only in the morning of his drop. One could not trust a man like that with serious responsibilties until he had finished his transit and had settled into his ultimate state.

They went into the serpent station together. Kurtz reached up as he passed the distilling apparatus, lightly caressing tubing and petcocks. His fingers were like a spider's legs, and the caress was astonishingly obscene. At the far end of the room stood a short, stocky man, dark-haired, black-browed, the station supervisor. Gio' Salamone. Kurtz made the introductions. Salamone grinned. "Lucky you," he said. "How did you manage to get assigned here?"

"They just sent me," Gundersen said.

"As somebody's practical joke," Kurtz suggested.

"I believe it," said Gundersen. "Everyone thought I was fibbing when I said I was sent here without applying." "A test of innocence," Kurtz murmured.

Salamone said, "Well, now that you're here, you'd better learn our basic rule. The basic rule is that when you leave this station, you never discuss what happens here with anybody else. *Capisce?* Now say to me, 'I swear by the Father, Son, and Holy Ghost, and also by Abraham, Isaac, Jacob, and Moses—' "

Kurtz choked with laughter.

Bewildered, Gundersen said, "That's an oath I've never heard before."

"Salamone's an Italian Jew," said Kurtz. "He's trying to cover all possibilities. Don't bother swearing, but he's right: what happens here isn't anybody else's business. Whatever you may have heard about the serpent station is probably true, but nevertheless tell no tales when you leave here." *Whang*. *Whang*. "Watch us carefully, now. We're going to call up our demons. Loose the amplifiers, Gio'."

Salamone seized a plastic sack of what looked like golden flour and hauled it toward the station's rear door. He scooped out a handful. With a quick upward heave he sent it into the air; the breeze instantly caught the tiny glittering grains and carried them aloft. Kurtz said. "He's just scattered a thousand microamplifiers into the jungle. In ten minutes they'll cover a radius of ten kilometers. They're tuned to pick up the frequencies of my guitar and Gio's flute, and the resonances go bouncing back and forth all over the place." Kurtz began to play, picking up a melody in mid-course. Salamone produced a short transverse flute and wove a melody of his own through the spaces in Kurtz's tune. Their playing became a stately sarabande, delicate, hypnotic, two or three figures repeated endlessly without variations in volume or pitch. For ten minutes nothing unusual occurred. Then Kurtz nodded toward the edge of the jungle. "They're coming," he whispered. "We're the original and authentic snake charmers."

Gundersen watched the serpents emerging from the forest. They were four times as long as a man, and as thick as a big man's arm. Undulating fins ran down their backs from end to end. Their skins were glossy, pale green, and evidently sticky, for the detritus of the forest floor stuck to them in places, bits of leaves and soil and crumpled petals. Instead of eyes, they had rows of platter-sized sensor spots flanking their rippling dorsal fins. Their heads were blunt; their mouths only slits, suitable merely for nibbling on gobbets of soil. Where nostrils might be, there protruded two slender quills as long as a man's thumb; these extended to five times that length in moments of stress or when the serpent was under attack, and yielded a blue fluid, a venom. Despite the size of the creatures, despite the arrival of perhaps thirty of them at once, Gundersen did not find them frightening, although he would certainly have been uneasy at the arrival of a platoon of pythons. These were not pythons. They were not even reptiles at all, but low-phylum creatures, actually giant worms. They were sluggish and of no apparent intelligence. But clearly they responded powerfully to the music. It had drawn them to the station, and now they writhed in a ghastly ballet, seeking the source of the sound. The first few were already entering the building.

"Do you play the guitar?" Kurtz asked. "Here—just keep the sound going. The tune's not important now." He thrust the instrument at Gundersen, who struggled with the fingerings a moment, then brought forth a lame, stumbling imitation of Kurtz's melody. Kurtz, meanwhile, was slipping a tubular pink cap over the head of the nearest serpent. When it was in place, the cap began rhythmic contractions; the serpent's writhings became momentarily more intense, its fin moved convulsively, its tail lashed the ground. Then it grew calm. Kurtz removed the cap and slid it over the head of another serpent, and another, and another.

He was milking them of venom. These creatures were deadly to native metabolic systems, so it was said; they never attacked, but when provoked they struck, and the poison was universally effective. But what was poison on Holman's World was a blessing on Earth. The venom of the jungle serpents was one of the Company's most profitable exports. Properly distilled, diluted, crystallized, purified, the juice served as a catalyst in limb-regeneration work. A dose of it softened the resistance of the human cell to change, insidiously corrupting the cytoplasm, leading it to induce the nucleus to switch on its genetic material. And so it greatly encouraged the reawakening of cell division, the replication of bodily parts, when a new arm or leg or face had to be grown. How or why it worked, Gundersen knew not, but he had seen the stuff in action during his training period, when a fellow trainee had lost both legs below the knee in a soarer accident. The drug made the flesh flow. It liberated the guardians of the body's coded pattern, easing the task of the genetic surgeons tenfold by sensitizing and stimulating the zone of regeneration. Those legs had grown back in six months.

Gundersen continued to strum the guitar, Salamone to play his flute. Kurtz to collect the venom. Mooing sounds came suddenly from the bush; a herd of nildoror evidently had been drawn by the music as well. Gundersen saw them lumber out of the underbrush and stand almost shyly by the border of the clearing, nine of them. After a moment they entered into a clumsy, lurching, ponderous dance. Their trunks waved in time to the music; their tails swung; their spiny crests revolved. "All done." Kurtz announced. "Five liters—a good haul." The serpents, milked, drifted into the forest as soon as the music ceased. The nildoror stayed a while longer, peering intently at the men inside the station, but finally they left also. Kurtz and Salamone instructed Gundersen in the techniques of distilling the precious fluid, making it ready for shipment to Earth.

And that was all. He could see nothing scandalous in what had happened, and did not understand why there had been so much sly talk at headquarters about this place, nor why Salamone had tried to wring an oath of silence from him. He dared not ask. Three days later they again summoned the serpents, again collected their venom, and again the whole process seemed unexceptionable to Gundersen. But soon he came to realize that Kurtz and Salamone were testing his reliability before initiating him into their mysteries.

In the third week of his stint at the serpent station they finally admitted him to the inner knowledge. The collection was done: the serpents had gone; a few nildoror, out of more than a dozen that had been attracted by that day's concert, still lingered outside the building. Gundersen realized that something unusual was about to happen when he saw Kurtz, after darting a sharp glance at Salamone, unhook a container of venom before it started on its route through the distilling apparatus. He poured it into a broad bowl that held at least a liter of fluid. On Earth, that much of the drug would be worth a year of Gundersen's salary as an assistant station agent. "Come with us," Kurtz said.

The three men stepped outside. At once three nildoror approached, behaving oddly, their spines upraised, their ears trembling. They seemed skittish and eager. Kurtz handed the bowl of raw venom to Salamone, who sipped from it and handed it back. Kurtz also drank. He gave the bowl to Gundersen, saying, "Take communion with us?"

Gundersen hesitated. Salamone said, "It's safe. It can't work on your nuclei when you take it internally."

Putting the bowl to his lips, Gundersen took a cautious swig. The venom was sweet but watery.

"—only on your brain," Salamone added.

Kurtz gently took the bowl from him and set it down on the ground. Now the largest nildor advanced and delicately dipped his trunk into it. Then the second nildor drank, and the third. The bowl now was empty.

Gundersen said, "If it's poisonous to native life—"

"Not when they drink it. Just when it's shot directly into the bloodstream," Salamone said.

"What happens now?"

"Wait," Kurtz said, "and make your soul receptive to any suggestions that arise."

Gundersen did not have to wait long. He felt a thickening at the base of his neck and a roughness about his face, and his arms seemed impossibly heavy. It seemed best to drop to his knees as the effect intensified. He turned toward Kurtz, seeking reassurance from those dark shining eyes, but Kurtz's eyes had already begun to flatten and expand, and his green and prehensile trunk nearly reached the ground. Salamone, too, had entered the metamorphosis, capering comically, jabbing the soil with his tusks. The thickening continued. Now Gundersen knew that he weighed several tons, and he tested his body's coordination, striding back and forth, learning how to move on four limbs. He went to the spring and sucked up water in his trunk. He rubbed his leathery hide against trees. He trumpeted bellowing sounds of joy in his hugeness. He joined with Kurtz and Salamone in a wild dance, making the ground quiver. The nildoror too were transformed; one had become Kurtz, one had become Salamone, one had become Gundersen, and the three former beasts moved in wild pirouettes, tumbling and toppling in their unfamiliarity with human ways. But Gundersen lost interest in what the nildoror were doing. He concentrated solely on his own experience. Somewhere at the core of his soul it terrified him to know that this change had come over him and he was doomed forever to live as a massive animal of the jungle, shredding bark and ripping branches; yet it was rewarding to have shifted bodies this way and to have access to an entirely new range of sensory data. His eyesight now was dimmed, and everything that he saw was engulfed in a furry halo, but there were compensations: he was able to sort odors by their directions and by their textures, and his hearing was immensely more sensitive. It was the equivalent of being able to see into the ultraviolet and the infrared. A dingy forest flower sent dizzying waves of sleek moist sweetness at him;

the click of insect-claws in underground tunnels was like a symphony for percussion. And the bigness of him! The ecstasy of carrying such a body! His transformed consciousness soared, swooped, rose high again. He trampled trees and praised himself for it in booming tones. He grazed and gorged. Then he sat for a while, perfectly still, and meditated on the existence of evil in the universe, asking himself why there should be such a thing, and indeed whether evil in fact existed as an objective phenomenon. His answers surprised and delighted him, and he turned to Kurtz to communicate his insights, but just then the effect of the venom began to fade with quite startling suddenness, and in a short while Gundersen felt altogether normal again. He was weeping, though, and he felt an anguish of shame, as though he had been flagrantly detected molesting a child. The three nildoror were nowhere in sight. Salamone picked up the bowl and went into the station. "Come," Kurtz said. "Let's go in too."

They would not discuss any of it with him. They had let him share in it, but they would not explain a thing, cutting him off sternly when he asked. The rite was hermetically private. Gundersen was wholly unable to evaluate the experience. Had his body actually turned into that of a nildor for an hour? Hardly. Well, then, had his mind, his soul, somehow migrated into the nildor's body? And had the nildor's soul, if nildoror had souls, gone into his? What kind of sharing, what sort of union of innernesses, had occurred in that clearing?

Three days afterward, Gundersen applied for a transfer out of the serpent station. In those days he was easily upset by the unknown. Kurtz's only reaction, when Gundersen announced he was leaving, was a short brutal chuckle. The normal tour of duty at the station was eight weeks, of which Gundersen had done less than half. He never again served a stint there.

Later, he gathered what gossip he could about the doings at the serpent station. He was told vague tales of sexual abominations in the grove, of couplings between Earthman and nildor, between Earthman and Earthman; he heard murmurs that those who habitually drank the venom underwent strange and terrible permanent changes of the body; he heard stories of how the nildoror elders in their private councils bitterly condemned the morbid practice of going to the serpent station to drink the stuff the Earthmen offered. But Gundersen did not know if any of these whispers were true. He found it difficult, in later years, to look Kurtz in the eye on the rare occasions when they met. Sometimes he found it difficult even to live with himself. In some peripheral way he had been tainted by his single hour of metamorphosis. He felt like a virgin who had stumbled into an orgy, and who had come away deflowered but yet ignorant of what had befallen her.

The phantoms faded. The sound of Kurtz's guitar diminished and was gone.

Srin'gahar said, "Shall we leave now?"

Gundersen slowly emerged from the ruined station. "Does anyone gather the juices of the serpents today?"

"Not here," said the nildor. He knelt. The Earthman mounted him, and in silence Srin'gahar carried him away, back to the path they had followed earlier.

Four

IN EARLY AFTERNOON they neared the nildoror encampment that was Gundersen's immediate goal. For most of the day they had been traveling across the broad coastal plain, but now the back of the land dipped sharply, for this far inland there was a long, narrow depression running from north to south, a deep rift between the central plateau and the coast. At the approach to this rift Gundersen saw the immense devastation of foliage that signaled the presence of a large nildoror herd within a few kilometers. A jagged scar ran through the forest from ground level to a point about twice a man's height.

Even the lunatic tropical fertility of this region could not keep up with the nildoror appetite; it took a year or more for such zones of defoliation to restore themselves after the herd had moved on. Yet despite the impact of the herd, the forest on all sides of the scar was even more close-knit here than on the coastal plain to the east. This was a jungle raised to the next higher power, damp, steamy, dark. The temperature was considerably higher in the valley than at the coast, and though the atmosphere could not possibly have been any more humid here, there was an almost tangible wetness about the air. The vegetation was different, too. On the plain the trees tended to have sharp, sometimes dangerously sharp, leaves. Here the foliage was rounded and fleshy, heavy sagging disks of dark blue that glistened voluptuously whenever stray shafts of sunlight pierced the forest canopy overhead.

Gundersen and his mount continued to descend, following the line of the grazing scar. Now they made their way along the route of a stream that flowed perversely inland; the soil was spongy and soft, and more often than not Srin'gahar walked knee-deep in mud. They were entering a wide circular basin at what seemed to be the lowest point in the entire region. Streams flowed into it on three or four sides, feeding a dark weed-covered lake at the center; and around the margin of the lake was Srin'gahar's herd. Gundersen saw several hundred nildoror grazing, sleeping, coupling, strolling.

"Put me down," he said, taking himself by surprise. "I'll walk beside you."

Wordlessly Srin'gahar allowed him to dismount.

Gundersen regretted his egalitarian impulse the moment he stepped down. The nildor's broad-padded feet were able to cope with the muddy floor; but Gundersen discovered that he had a tendency to begin to sink in if he remained in one place more than a moment. But he would not remount now. Every step was a struggle, but he struggled. He was tense and uncertain, too, of the reception he would get here, and he was hungry as well, having eaten nothing on the long journey but a few bitterfruits plucked from passing trees. The closeness of the climate made each breath a battle for him. He was greatly relieved when the footing became easier a short distance down the slope. Here, a webwork of spongy plants spreading out from the lake underwove the mud to form a firm, if not altogether reassuring, platform a few centimeters down.

Srin'gahar raised his trunk and sounded a trumpetblast of greeting to the encampment. A few of the nildoror replied in kind. To Gundersen, Srin'gahar said, "The many-born one stands at the edge of the lake, friend of my journey. You see him, yes, in that group? Shall I lead you now to him?"

"Please," said Gundersen.

The lake was congested with drifting vegetation. Humped masses of it broke the surface everywhere: leaves like horns of plenty, cup-shaped spore-bodies, ropy tangled stems, everything dark blue against the lighter blue-green of the water. Through this maze of tight-packed flora there slowly moved huge semiaquatic mammals, half a dozen malidaror, whose tubular yellowish bodies were almost totally submerged. Only the rounded bulges of their backs and the jutting periscopes of their stalked eyes were in view, and now and then a pair of cavernous snorting nostrils. Gundersen could see the immense swaths that the malidaror had cut through the vegetation in this day's feeding, but at the far side of the lake the wounds were beginning to close as new growth hastened to fill the fresh gaps.

Gundersen and Srin'gahar went down toward the water. Suddenly the wind shifted, and Gundersen had a whiff of the lake's fragrance. He coughed; it was like breathing the fumes of a distillery vat. The lake was in ferment. Alcohol was a by-product of the respiration of these water-plants, and, having no outlet, the lake became one large tub of brandy. Both water and alcohol evaporated from it at a rapid pace, making the surrounding air not only steamy but potent; and during centuries when evaporation of water had exceeded the inflow from the streams, the proof of the residue had steadily risen. When the Company ruled this planet, such lakes had been the undoing of more than one agent, Gundersen knew.

The nildoror appeared to pay little heed to him as he came near them. Gundersen was aware that every member of the encampment was actually watching him closely, but they pretended to casualness and went about their business. He was puzzled to see a dozen brush shelters flanking one of the streams. Nildoror did not live in dwellings of any sort; the climate made it unnecessary, and besides they were incapable of constructing anything, having no organs of manipulation other than the three "fingers" at the tips of their trunks. He studied the crude lean-tos in bewilderment, and after a moment it dawned on him that he had seen structures of this sort before: they were the huts of sulidoror. The puzzle deepened. Such close association between the nildoror and the carnivorous bipeds of the mist country was unknown to him. Now he saw the sulidoror themselves, perhaps twenty of them, sitting crosslegged inside their huts. Slaves? Captives? Friends of the tribe? None of those ideas made sense.

"That is our many-born," Srin'gahar said, indicating with a wave of his trunk a seamed and venerable nildor in the midst of a group by the lakeshore.

Gundersen felt a surge of awe, inspired not only by the great age of the creature, but by the knowledge that this ancient beast, blue-gray with years, must have taken part several times in the unimaginable rites of the rebirth ceremony. The many-born one had journeyed beyond the barrier of spirit that held Earthmen back. Whatever nirvana the rebirth ceremony offered, this being had tasted it, and Gundersen had not, and that crucial distinction of experience made Gundersen's courage shrivel as he approached the leader of the herd.

A ring of courtiers surrounded the old one. They were gray-skinned and wrinkled, too: a congregation of seniors. Younger nildoror, of the generation of Srin'gahar, kept a respectful distance. There were no immature nildoror in the encampment at all. No Earthman had ever seen a young nildor. Gundersen had been told that the nildoror were always born in the mist country, in the home country of the sulidoror, and apparently they remained in close seclusion there until they had reached the nildoror equivalent of adolescence, when they migrated to the jungles of the tropics. He also had heard that every nildor hoped to go back to the mist country when its time had come to die. But he did not know if such things were true. No one did.

The ring opened, and Gundersen found himself facing the many-born one. Protocol demanded that Gundersen speak first; but he faltered, dizzied by tension perhaps, or perhaps by the fumes of the lake, and it was an endless moment before he pulled himself together.

He said at last, "I am Edmund Gundersen of the first birth, and I wish you joy of many rebirths, O wisest one."

Unhurriedly the nildor swung his vast head to one side, sucked up a snort of water from the lake, and squirted it into his mouth. Then he rumbled, "You are known to us, Edmundgundersen, from days past. You kept the big house of the Company at Fire Point in the Sea of Dust."

The nildor's sharpness of memory astonished and distressed him. If they remembered him so well, what chance did he have to win favors from these people? They owed him no kindnesses.

"I was there, yes, a long time ago," he said tightly.

"Not so long ago. Ten turnings is not a long time." The nildor's heavy-lidded eyes closed, and it appeared for some moments as though the many-born one had fallen asleep. Then the nildor said, eyes still closed, "I am Vol'himyor of the seventh birth. Will you come into the water with me? I grow tired easily on the land in this present birth of mine."

Without waiting, Vol'himyor strode into the lake, swimming slowly to a point some forty meters from shore and floating there, submerged up to the shoulders. A malidar that had been browsing on the weeds in that part of the lake went under with a bubbling murmur of discontent and reappeared far away. Gundersen knew that he had no choice but to follow the many-born one. He stripped off his clothing and walked forward.

The tepid water rose about him. Not far out, the spongy matting of fibrous stems below ground level gave way to soft warm mud beneath Gundersen's bare feet. He felt the occasional movement of small many-legged things under his soles. The roots of the water-plants swirled whip-like about his legs, and the black bubbles of alcohol that came up from the depths and burst on the surface almost stifled him with their release of vapor. He pushed plants aside, forcing his way through them with the greatest difficulty, and feeling a great relief when his feet lost contact with the mud. Quickly he paddled himself out to Vol'himyor. The surface of the water was clear there, thanks to the malidar. In the dark depths of the lake, though, unknown creatures moved to and fro, and every few moments something slippery and quick slithered along Gundersen's body. He forced himself to ignore such things.

Vol'himyor, still seemingly asleep, murmured, "You have been gone from this world for many turnings, have you not?"

"After the Company relinquished its rights here, I returned to my own world," said Gundersen.

Even before the nildor's eyelids parted, even before the round yellow eyes fixed coldly on him, Gundersen was aware that he had blundered.

"Your Company never had rights here to relinquish," said the nildor in the customary flat, neutral way. "Is this not so?"

"It is so," Gundersen conceded. He searched for a graceful correction and finally said, "After the Company relinquished possession of this planet, I returned to my own world."

"Those words are more nearly true. Why, then, have you come back here?"

"Because I love this place and wish to see it again."

"Is it possible for an Earthman to feel love for Belzagor?"

"An Earthman can, yes."

"An Earthman can become *captured* by Belzagor," Vol'himyor said with more than usual slowness. "An Earthman may find that his soul has been seized by the forces of this planet and is held in thrall. But I doubt that an Earthman can feel love for this planet, as I understand your understanding of love."

"I yield the point, many-born one. My soul has become captured by Belzagor. I could not help but return."

"You are quick to yield such points."

"I have no wish to give offense."

"Commendable tact. And what will you do here on this world that has seized your soul?"

"Travel to many parts of your world," said Gundersen. "I wish particularly to go to the mist country."

"Why there?"

"It is the place that captures me most deeply."

"That is not an informative answer," the nildor said.

"I can give no other."

"What thing has captured you there?"

"The beauty of the mountains rising out of the mist. The sparkle of sunlight on a clear, cold, bright day. The splendor of the moons against a field of glittering snow."

"You are quite poetic," said Vol'himyor.

Gundersen could not tell if he were being praised or mocked.

He said, "Under present law, I must have the permission of a many-born one to enter the mist country. So I come to make application to you for such permission."

"You are fastidious in your respect for our law, my once-born friend. Once it was different with you."

Gundersen bit his lip. He felt something crawling up his calf, down in the depths of the lake, but he compelled himself to stare serenely at the many-born one. Choosing his words with care, he said, "Sometimes we are slow to understand the nature of others, and we give offense without knowing that we do so."

"It is so."

"But then understanding comes," Gundersen said, "and one feels remorse for the deeds of the past, and one hopes that one may be forgiven for his sins."

"Forgiveness depends on the quality of the remorse," said Vol'himyor, "and also on the quality of the sins."

"I believe my failings are known to you."

"They are not forgotten," said the nildor.

"I believe also that in your creed the possibility of personal redemption is not unknown."

"True. True."

"Will you allow me to make amends for my sins of the past against your people, both known and unknown?"

"Making amends for unknown sins is meaningless," said the nildor. "But in any case we seek no apologies. Your redemption from sin is your own concern, not ours. Perhaps you will find that redemption here, as you hope. I sense already a welcome change in your soul, and it will count heavily in your favor."

"I have your permission to go north, then?" Gundersen asked.

"Not so fast. Stay with us a while as our guest. We must think about this. You may go to shore, now."

The dismissal was clear. Gundersen thanked the many-born one for his patience, not without some self-satisfaction at the way he had handled the interview. He had always displayed proper deference toward many-born ones—even a really Kiplingesque imperialist knew enough to show respect for venerable tribal leaders—but in Company days it had never been more than a charade for him, a put-on show of humility, since ultimate power resided with the Company's sector agent, not with any nildor no matter how holy. Now, of course, the old nildor really did have the power to keep him out of the mist country, and might even see some poetic justice in banning him from it. But Gundersen felt that his deferential and apologetic attitude had been reasonably sincere just now, and that some of that sincerity had been communicated to Vol'himyor. He knew that he could not deceive the many-born one into thinking that an old Company hand like himself was suddenly eager to grovel before the former victims of Earth's expansionism; but unless some show of earnestness did come through, he stood no chance at all of gaining the permission he needed.

Abruptly, when Gundersen was still a good distance from shore, something hit him a tremendous blow between the shoulders and flung him, stunned and gasping, face forward into the water.

As he went under, the thought crossed his mind that Vol'himyor had treacherously come up behind him and lashed him with his trunk. Such a blow could easily be fatal if aimed with real malice. Spluttering, his mouth full of the lake's liquor, his arms half numbed by the impact of the blow, Gundersen warily surfaced, expecting to find the old nildor looming above him ready to deliver the coup de grace.

He opened his eyes, with some momentary trouble focusing them. No, there was the many-born one far away across the water, looking in another direction. And then Gundersen felt a curious prickly premonition and got his head down just in time to avoid being decapitated by whatever it was that had hit him before. Huddling nose-deep in the water, he saw it swing by overhead, a thick yellowish rod like a boom out of control. Now he heard thunderous shrieks of pain and felt widening ripples sweeping across the lake. He glanced around.

A dozen sulidoror had entered the water and were killing a malidar. They had harpooned the colossal beast with sharpened sticks; now the malidar thrashed and coiled in its final agonies, and it was the mighty tail of the animal that had knocked Gundersen over. The hunters had fanned out in the shallows, waist-deep, their thick fur bedraggled and matted. Each group grasped the line of one harpoon, and they were gradually drawing the malidar toward shore. Gundersen was no longer in danger, but he continued to stay low in the water, catching his breath, rotating his shoulders to assure himself that no bones were broken. The malidar's tail must have given him the merest tip-flick the first time; he would surely have been destroyed the second time that tail came by, if he had not ducked. He was beginning to ache, and he felt half drowned by the water he had gulped. He wondered when he would start to get drunk.

Now the sulidoror had beached their prey. Only the malidar's tail and thick web-footed hind legs lay in the water, moving fitfully. The rest of the animal, tons of it, stretching five times the length of a man, was up on shore, and the sulidoror were methodically driving long stakes into it, one through each of the forelimbs and several into the broad wedge-shaped head. A few nildoror were watching the operation in mild curiosity. Most ignored it. The remaining malidaror continued to browse in the woods as though nothing had happened.

A final thrust of a stake severed the malidar's spinal column. The beast quivered and lay still.

Gundersen hurried from the water, swimming quickly, then wading through the unpleasantly voluptuous mud, at last stumbling out onto the beach. His knees suddenly failed him and he toppled forward, trembling, choking, puking. A thin stream of fluid burst from his lips. Afterward he rolled to one side and watched the sulidoror cutting gigantic blocks of pale pink meat from the malidar's sides and passing them around. Other sulidoror were coming from the huts to share the feast. Gundersen shivered. He was in a kind of shock, and a few minutes passed before he realized that the cause of his shock was not only the blow he had received and the water he had swallowed, but also the knowledge that an act of violence had been committed in front of a herd of nildoror, and the nildoror did not seem at all disturbed. He had imagined that these peaceful, nonbelligerent creatures would react in horror to the slaughter of a malidar. But they simply did not care. The shock Gundersen felt was the shock of disillusionment.

A sulidor approached him and stood over him. Gundersen stared up uneasily at the towering shaggy figure. The sulidor held in its forepaws a gobbet of malidar meat the size of Gundersen's head.

"For you," said the sulidor in the nildoror language. "You eat with us?"

It did not wait for a reply. It tossed the slab of flesh to the ground next to Gundersen and rejoined its fellows. Gundersen's stomach writhed. He had no lust for raw meat just now.

The beach was suddenly very silent.

They were all watching him, sulidoror and nildoror both.

Five

SHAKILY GUNDERSEN GOT to his feet. He sucked warm air into his lungs and bought a little time by crouching at the lake's edge to wash his face. He found his discarded clothing and consumed a few minutes by getting it on. Now he felt a little better; but the problem of the raw meat remained. The sulidoror, enjoying their feast, rending and tearing flesh and gnawing on bones, nevertheless frequently looked his way to see whether he would accept their hospitality. The nildoror, who of course had not touched the meat themselves, also seemed curious about his decision. If he refused the meat, would he offend the sulidoror? If he ate it, would he stamp himself as bestial in the eyes of the nildoror? He concluded that it was best to force some of the meat into him, as a gesture of good will toward the menacing-looking bipeds. The nildoror, after all, did not seem troubled that the sulidoror were eating meat; why should it bother them if an Earthman, a known carnivore, did the same?

He would eat the meat. But he would eat it as an Earthman would.

He ripped some leaves from the water-plant and spread them out to form a mat; he placed the meat on this. From his tunic he took his fusion torch, which he adjusted for wide aperture, low intensity, and played on the meat until its outer surface was charred and bubbling. With a narrower beam he cut the cooked meat into chunks he could manage. Then, squatting cross-legged, he picked up a chunk and bit into it.

The meat was soft and cheesy, interlaced by tough stringlike masses forming an intricate grid. By will alone Gundersen succeeded in getting three pieces down. When he decided he had had enough, he rose, called out his thanks to the sulidoror, and knelt by the side of the lake to scoop up some of the water. He needed a chaser.

During all this time no one spoke to him or approached him.

The nildoror had all left the water, for night was approaching. They had settled down in several groups well back from the shore. The feast of the sulidoror continued noisily, but was nearing its end; already several small scavenger-beasts had joined the party, and were at work at the lower half of the malidar's body while the sulidoror finished the other part.

Gundersen looked about for Srin'gahar. There were things he wished to ask.

It still troubled him that the nildoror had accepted the killing in the lake so coolly. He realized that he had somehow always regarded the nildoror as more noble than the other big beasts of this planet because they did not take life except under supreme provocation, and sometimes not even then. Here was an intelligent race exempt from the sin of Cain. And Gundersen saw in that a corollary: that the nildoror, because they did not kill, would look upon killing as a detestable act. Now he knew that his reasoning was faulty and even naïve. The nildoror did not kill simply because they were not eaters of meat; but the moral superiority that he had attributed to them on that score must in fact be a product of his own guilty imagination.

The night came on with tropic swiftness. A single moon glimmered. Gundersen saw a nildor he took to be Srin'gahar, and went to him.

"I have a question, Srin'gahar, friend of my journey," Gundersen began. "When the sulidoror entered the water—"

The nildor said gravely, "You make a mistake. I am Thali'vanoom of the third birth."

Gundersen mumbled an apology and turned away, aghast. What a typically Earthman blunder, he thought. He remembered his old sector chief making the same blunder a dozen dozen times, hopelessly confusing one nildor with another and muttering angrily, "Can't tell one of these big bastards from the next! Why don't they wear badges?" The ultimate insult, the failure to recognize the natives as individuals. Gundersen had always made it a point of honor to avoid such gratuitous insults. And so, here, at this delicate time when he depended wholly on winning the favor of the nildoror—

He approached a second nildor, and saw just at the last moment that this one too was not Srin'gahar. He backed off as gracefully as he could. On the third attempt he finally found his traveling companion. Srin'gahar sat placidly against a narrow tree, his thick legs folded beneath his body. Gundersen put his question to him and Srin'gahar said, "Why should the sight of violent death shock us? Malidaror have no *g'rakh,* after all. And it is obvious that sulidoror must eat."

"No *g'rakh*?" Gundersen said. "This is a word I do not know."

"The quality that separates the souled from the unsouled," Srin'gahar explained. "Without *g'rakh* a creature is but a beast."

"Do sulidoror have *g'rakh*?"

"Of course."

"And nildoror also, naturally. But malidaror don't. What about Earthmen?"

"It is amply clear that Earthmen have *g'rakh.*"

"And one may freely kill a creature which lacks that quality?"

"If one has the need to do so, yes," said Srin'gahar. "These are elementary matters. Have you no such concepts on your own world?"

"On my world," said Gundersen, "there is only one species that has been granted *g'rakh,* and so perhaps we give such matters too little thought. We know that whatever is not of our own kind must be lacking in *g'rakh.*"

"And so, when you come to another world, you have difficulty in accepting the presence of *g'rakh* in other beings?" Srin'gahar asked. "You need not answer. I understand."

"May I ask another question?" said Gundersen. "Why are there sulidoror here?"

"We allow them to be here."

"In the past, in the days when the Company ruled Belzagor, the sulidoror never went outside the mist country."

"We did not allow them to come here then."

"But now you do. Why?"

"Because now it is easier for us to do so. Difficulties stood in the way at earlier times."

"What kind of difficulties?" Gundersen persisted.

Softly Srin'gahar said, "You will have to ask that of someone who has been born more often than I. I am once-born, and many things are as strange to me as they are to you. Look, another moon is in the sky! At the third moon we shall dance."

Gundersen looked up and saw the tiny white disk moving rapidly, low in sky, seemingly skimming the fringe of the treetops. Belzagor's five moons were a random assortment, the closest one just outside Roche's Limit, the farthest so distant it was visible only to sharp eyes on a clear night. At any given time two or three moons were in the night sky, but the fourth and fifth moons had such eccentric orbits that they could never be seen at all from vast regions of the planet, and passed over most other zones no more than three or four times a year. One night each year all five moons could be seen at once, just along a band ten kilometers wide running at an angle of about forty degrees to the equator from northeast to southwest. Gundersen had experienced the Night of Five Moons only a single time.

The nildoror were starting to move toward the lakeshore now.

The third moon appeared, spinning retrograde into view from the south.

So he was going to see them dance again. He had witnessed their ceremonies once before, early in his career, when he was stationed at Shangri-la Falls in the northern tropics. That night the nildoror had massed just upstream of the falls, on both banks of Madden's River, and for hours after dark their blurred cries could be heard even above the roar of the water. And finally Kurtz, who was also stationed at Shangri-la then, said, "Come, let's watch the show!" and led Gundersen out into the night. This was six months before the episode at the serpent station, and Gundersen did not then realize how strange Kurtz was. But he realized it quickly enough after Kurtz joined the nildoror in their dance. The huge beasts were clustered in loose semicircles, stamping back and forth, trumpeting piercingly, shaking the ground, and suddenly there was Kurtz out there among them, arms upflung, bare chest beaded with sweat and shining in the moonslight, dancing as intensely as any of them, crying out in great booming roars, stamping his feet, tossing his head. And the nildoror were forming a group around him, giving him plenty of space, letting him enter fully into the frenzy, now running toward him, now backing away, a systole and diastole of ferocious power. Gundersen stood awed, and did not move when Kurtz called to him to join the dance. He watched for what seemed like hours, hypnotized by the boom boom *boom* boom of the dancing nildoror, until in the end he broke from his trance, and searched for Kurtz and found him still in ceaseless motion, a gaunt bony skeletonic figure jerking puppet-like on invisible strings, looking fragile despite his extreme height as he moved within the circle of colossal nildoror. Kurtz could neither hear Gundersen's words nor take note of his presence, and finally Gundersen went back to the station alone. In the morning he found Kurtz, looking spent and worn, slumped on the bench overlooking the waterfall. Kurtz merely said, "You should have stayed. You should have danced."

Anthropologists had studied these rites. Gundersen had looked up the literature, learning what little there was to learn. Evidently the dance was preceded and surrounded by drama, a spoken episode akin to Earth's medieval mystery plays, a theatrical reenactment of some supremely important nildoror myth, serving both as mode of entertainment and as ecstatic religious experience. Unfortunately the language of the drama was an obsolete liturgical tongue, not a word of which could be understood by an Earthman, and the nildoror, who had not hesitated to instruct their first Earthborn visitors in their relatively simple modern language, had never offered any clue to the nature of the other one. The anthropological observers had noted one point which Gundersen now found cheering: invariably, within a few days after the performance of this particular rite, groups of nildoror from the herd performing it would set out for the mist country, presumably to undergo rebirth.

He wondered if the rite might be some ceremony of purification, some means of entering a state of grace before undergoing rebirth.

The nildoror all had gathered, now, beside the lake. Srin'gahar was one of the last to go. Gundersen sat alone on the slope above the basin, watching the massive forms assembling. The contrary motions of the moons fragmented the shadows of the nildoror, and the cold light from above turned their smooth green hides into furrowed black cloaks. Looking over to his left, Gundersen saw the sulidoror squatting before their huts, excluded from the ceremony but apparently not forbidden to view it.

In the silence came a low, clear, forceful flow of words. He strained to hear, hoping to catch some clue to the meaning, seeking a magical gateway that would let him burst through into an understanding of that secret language. But no understanding came. Vol'himyor was the speaker, the old many-born one, reciting words clearly familiar to everyone at the lake, an invocation, an introit. Then came a long interval of silence, and then came a response from a second nildor at the opposite end of the group, who exactly duplicated the rhythms and sinuosities of Vol'himyor's utterance. Silence again; and then a reply from Vol'himyor, spoken more crisply. Back and forth the center of the service moved, and the interplay between the two celebrants became what was for nildoror a surprisingly quick exchange of dialogue. About every tenth line the herd at large repeated what a celebrant had said, sending dark reverberations through the night.

After perhaps ten minutes of this the voice of a third solo nildor was heard. Vol'himyor made reply. A fourth speaker took up the recitation. Now isolated lines were coming in rapid bursts from many members of the congregation. No cue was missed; no nildor trampled on another's lines. Each seemed intuitively to know when to speak, when to stay silent. The tempo accelerated. The ceremony had become a mosaic of brief utterances blared forth from every part of the group in a random rotation. A few of the nildoror were up and moving slowly in place, lifting their feet, putting them down.

Lightning speared through the sky. Despite the closeness of the atmosphere, Gundersen felt a chill. He saw himself as a wanderer on a prehistoric Earth, spying on some grotesque conclave of mastodons. All the things of man seemed infinitely far away now. The drama was reaching some sort of climax. The nildoror were bellowing, stamping, calling to one another with tremendous snorts. They were taking up formations, assembling in aisled rows. Still there came utterances and responses, antiphonal amplifications of words heavy with strange significance. The air grew more steamy. Gundersen could no longer hear individual words, only rich deep chords of massed grunts, ah ah *ah* ah, ah ah *ah* ah, the old rhythm that he remembered from the night at Shangri-la Falls. It was a breathy, gasping sound now, ecstatic, an endless chuffing pattern of exhalations, ah ah *ah* ah, ah ah *ah* ah, ah ah *ah* ah, with scarcely a break between each group of four beats, and the whole jungle seemed to echo with it. The nildoror had no musical instruments whatever, yet to Gundersen it appeared that vast drums were pounding out that hypnotically intense rhythm. Ah ah *ah* ah. Ah ah *ah* ah. AH AH *AH* AH! AH AH *AH* AH!

And the nildoror were dancing.

Down below on the margin of the lake moved scores of great shadowy shapes, prancing like gazelles, two running steps forward, stamp down hard on the third step, regain the balance on the fourth. The universe trembled. Boom boom *boom* boom, boom boom *boom* boom. The earlier phase of the ceremony, the dramatic dialogue, which might have been some sort of subtle philosophical disquisition, had given way totally to this primeval pounding, this terrifying shuffling of gigantic elephantine bodies. Boom boom *boom* boom. Gundersen looked to his left and saw the sulidoror entranced, hairy heads switching back and forth in the rhythm of the dance; but not one of the bipeds had risen from the cross-legged posture. They were content to rock and nod, and now and then to pound their elbows on the ground.

Gundersen was cut off from his own past, even from a

sense of his own kinship to his species. Disjointed memories floated up. Again he was at the serpent station, a prisoner of the hallucinatory venom, feeling himself transformed into a nildor and capering thickly in the grove. Again he stood by the bank of the great river, seeing another performance of this very dance. And also he remembered nights spent in the safety of Company stations deep in the forest, among his own kind, when they had listened to the sound of stamping feet in the distance. All those other times Gundersen had drawn back from whatever strangeness this planet was offering him; he had transferred out of the serpent station rather than taste the venom a second time, he had refused Kurtz's invitation to join the dance, he had remained within the stations when the rhythmic poundings began in the forest. But tonight he felt little allegiance to mankind. He found himself longing to join that black and incomprehensible frenzy at the lakeshore. Something monstrous was running free within him, liberated by the incessant repetition of that boom boom *boom* boom. But what right had he to caper Kurtzlike in an alien ceremony? He did not intrude on their ritual.

Yet he discovered that he was walking down the spongy slope toward the place where the massed nildoror cavorted.

If he could think of them only as leaping, snorting elephants it would be all right. If he could think of them even as savages kicking up a row it would be all right. But the suspicion was unavoidable that this ceremony of words and dancing held intricate meanings for these people, and that was the worst of it. They might have thick legs and short necks and long dangling trunks, but that did not make them elephants, for their triple tusks and spiny crests and alien anatomies said otherwise; and they might be lacking in all technology, lacking even in a written language, but that did not make them savages, for the complexity of their minds said otherwise. They were creatures who possessed *g'rakh*. Gundersen remembered how he had innocently attempted to instruct the nildoror in the arts of terrestrial culture, in an effort to help them "improve" themselves; he had wanted to humanize them, to lift their spirits upward, but nothing had come of that, and now he found his own spirit being drawn—downward?—certainly to their level, wherever that might lie. Boom boom *boom* boom. His feet hesitantly traced out the four-step as he continued down the slope toward the lake. Did he dare? Would they crush him as blasphemous?

They had let Kurtz dance. They had let Kurtz dance.

It had been a different latitude, a long time ago, and other nildoror had been involved, but they had let Kurtz dance.

"Yes," a nildor called to him. "Come, dance with us!"

Was it Vol'himyor? Was it Srin'gahar? Was it Thali'vanoom of the third birth? Gundersen did not know which of them had spoken. In the darkness, in the sweaty haze, he could not see clearly, and all these giant shapes looked identical. He reached the bottom of the slope. Nildoror were everywhere about him, tracing out passages in their private journeys from point to point on the lakeshore. Their bodies emitted acrid odors, which, mixing with the fumes of the lake, choked and dizzied him. He heard several of them say to him, "Yes, yes, dance with us!"

And he danced.

He found an open patch of marshy soil and laid claim to it, moving forward, then backward, covering and recovering his one little tract in his fervor. No nildoror trespassed on him. His head tossed; his eyes rolled; his arms dangled; his body swayed and rocked; his feet carried him untiringly. Now he sucked in the thick air. Now he cried out in strange tongues. His skin was on fire; he stripped away his clothing, but it made no difference. Boom boom *boom* boom. Even now, a shred of his old detachment was left, enough so that he could marvel at the spectacle of himself dancing naked amid a herd of giant alien beasts. Would they, in their ultimate transports of passion, sweep in over his plot and crush him into the muck? Surely it was dangerous to stay here in the heart of the herd. But he stayed. Boom boom *boom* boom, again, again, yet again. As he whirled he looked out over the lake, and by sparkling refracted moonslight he saw the malidaror placidly munching the weeds, heedless of the frenzy on land. They are without *g'rakh*, he thought. They are beasts, and when they die their leaden spirits go downward to the earth. Boom. Boom. BOOM. Boom.

He became aware that glossy shapes were moving along the ground, weaving warily between the rows of dancing nildoror. The serpents! This music of pounding feet had summoned them from the dense glades where they lived.

The nildoror seemed wholly unperturbed that these deadly worms moved among them. A single stabbing thrust of the two spiny quills would bring even a mighty nildor toppling down; but no matter. The serpents were welcome, it appeared. They glided toward Gundersen, who knew he was in no mortal danger from their venom, but who did not seek another encounter with it. He did not break the stride of his dance, though, as five of the thick pink creatures wriggled past him. They did not touch him.

The serpents passed through, and were gone. And still the uproar continued. And still the ground shook. Gundersen's heart hammered, but he did not pause. He gave himself up fully, blending with those about him, sharing as deeply as he was able to share it the intensity of the experience.

The moons set. Early streaks of dawn stained the sky.

Gundersen became aware that he no longer could hear the thunder of stamping feet. He danced alone. About him, the nildoror had settled down, and their voices again could be heard, in that strange unintelligible litany. They spoke quietly but with great passion. He could no longer follow the patterns of their words; everything merged into an echoing rumble of tones, without definition, without shape. Unable to halt, he jerked and twisted through his obsessive gyration until the moment that he felt the first heat of the morning sun.

Then he fell exhausted, and lay still, and slipped down easily into sleep.

Six

WHEN HE WOKE it was some time after midday. The normal life of the encampment had resumed; a good many of the nildoror were in the lake, a few were munching on the vegetation at the top of the slope, and most were resting in the shade. The only sign of last night's frenzy was in the spongy turf near the lakeshore, which was terribly scuffed and torn.

Gundersen felt stiff and numb. Also he was abashed, with the embarrassment of one who has thrown himself too eagerly into someone else's special amusement. He could hardly believe that he had done what he knew himself to have done. In his shame he felt an immediate impulse to leave the encampment at once, before the nildoror could show him their contempt for an Earthman capable of making himself a thrall to their festivity, capable of allowing himself to be beguiled by their incantations. But he shackled the thought, remembering that he had a purpose in coming here.

He limped down to the lake and waded out until its water came up to his breast. He soaked a while, and washed away the sweat of the night before. Emerging, he found his clothing and put it on.

A nildor came to him and said, "Vol'himyor will speak to you now."

The many-born one was halfway up the slope. Coming before him, Gundersen could not find the words of any of the greetings formulas, and simply stared raggedly at the old nildor until Vol'himyor said, "You dance well, my once-born friend. You dance with joy. You dance with love. You dance like a nildor, do you know that?"

"It is not easy for me to understand what happened to me last night." said Gundersen.

"You proved to us that our world has captured your spirit."

"Was it offensive to you that an Earthman danced among you?"

"If it had been offensive," said Vol'himyor slowly, "you would not have danced among us." There was a long silence. Then the nildor said, "We will make a treaty, we two. I will give you permission to go into the mist country. Stay there until you are ready to come out. But when you return, bring with you the Earthman known as Cullen, and offer him to the northernmost encampment of nildoror, the first of my people that you find. Is this agreed?"

"Cullen?" Gundersen asked. Across his mind flared the image of a short broad-faced man with fine golden hair and mild green eyes. "Cedric Cullen, who was here when I was here?"

"The same man."

"He worked with me when I was at the station in the Sea of Dust."

"He lives now in the mist country," Vol'himyor said, "having gone there without permission. We want him."

"What has he done?"

"He is guilty of a grave crime. Now he has taken sanctuary among the sulidoror, where we are unable to gain access to him. It would be a violation of our covenant with them if we removed this man ourselves. But we may ask you to do it."

Gundersen frowned. "You won't tell me the nature of his crime?"

"Does it matter? We want him. Our reasons are not trifling ones. We request you to bring him to us."

"You're asking one Earthman to seize another and turn him in for punishment," said Gundersen. "How am I to know where justice lies in this affair?"

"Under the treaty of relinquishment, are we not the arbiters of justice on this world?" asked one nildor.

Gundersen admitted that this was so.

"Then we hold the right to deal with Cullen as he deserves," Vol'himyor said.

That did not, of course, make it proper for Gundersen to act as catspaw in handing his old comrade over to the nildoror. But Vol'himyor's implied threat was clear: do as we wish, or we grant you no favors.

Gundersen said, "What punishment will Cullen get if he falls into your custody?"

"Punishment? Punishment? Who speaks of punishment?"

"If the man's a criminal—"

"We wish to purify him," said the many-born one. "We desire to cleanse his spirit. We do not regard that as punishment."

"Will you injure him physically in any way?"

"It is not to be thought."

"Will you end his life?"

"Can you mean such a thing? Of course not."

"Will you imprison him?"

"We will keep him in custody," said Vol'himyor, "for however long the rite of purification takes. I do not think it will take long. He will swiftly be freed, and he will be grateful to us."

"I ask you once more to tell me the nature of his crime."

"He will tell you that himself," the nildor said. "It is not necessary for me to make his confession for him."

Gundersen considered all aspects of the matter. Shortly he said, "I agree to our treaty, many-born one, but only if I may add several clauses."

"Go on."

"If Cullen will not tell me the nature of his crime, I am released from my obligation to hand him over."

"Agreed."

"If the sulidoror object to my taking Cullen out of the mist country, I am released from my obligation also."

"They will not object. But agreed."

"If Cullen must be subdued by violence in order to bring him forth, I am released."

The nildor hesitated a moment. "Agreed," he said finally.

"I have no other conditions to add."

"Then our treaty is made," Vol'himyor said. "You may begin your northward journey today. Five of our once-born ones must also travel to the mist country, for their time of rebirth has come, and if you wish they will accompany you and safeguard you along the way. Among them is Srin'gahar, whom you already know."

"Will it be troublesome for them to have me with them?"

"Srin'gahar has particularly requested the privilege of serving as your guardian," said Vol'himyor. "But we would not compel you to accept his aid, if you would rather make your journey alone."

"It would be an honor to have his company," Gundersen said.

"So be it, then."

A senior nildor summoned Srin'gahar and the four others who would be going toward rebirth. Gundersen was gratified at this confirmation of the existing data: once more the frenzied dance of the nildoror had preceded the departure of a group bound for rebirth.

It pleased him, too, to know that he would have a nildoror escort on the way north. There was only one dark aspect to the treaty, that which involved Cedric Cullen. He wished he had not sworn to barter another Earthman's freedom for his own safe-conduct pass. But perhaps Cullen had done something really loathsome, something that merited punishment—or purification, as Vol'himyor put it. Gundersen did not understand how that normally sunny man could have become a criminal and a fugitive, but Cullen had lived on this world a long time, and the strangeness of alien worlds ultimately corroded even the brightest souls. In any case, Gundersen felt that he had opened enough honorable exits for himself if he needed to escape from his treaty with Vol'himyor.

Srin'gahar and Gundersen went aside to plan their route. "Where in the mist country do you intend to go?" the nildor asked.

"It does not matter. I just want to enter it. I suppose I'll have to go wherever Cullen is."

"Yes. But we do not know exactly where he is, so we will have to wait until we are there to learn it. Do you have special places to visit on the way north?"

"I want to stop at the Earthman stations," Gundersen said. "Particularly at Shangri-la Falls. So my idea is that we'll follow Madden's River northwestward, and—"

"These names are unknown to me."

"Sorry. I guess they've all reverted back to nildororu names. And I don't know those. But wait—" Seizing a stick, Gundersen scratched a hasty but serviceable map of Belzagor's western hemisphere in the mud. Across the waist of the disk he drew the thick swath of the tropics. At the right side he gouged out a curving bite to indicate the ocean; on the left he outlined the Sea of Dust. Above and below the band of the tropics he drew the thinner lines representing the northern and southern mist zones, and beyond them he indicated the gigantic icecaps. He marked the spaceport and the hotel at the coast with an X, and cut a wiggly line up from there, clear across the tropics into the northern mist country, to show Madden's River. At the midway point of the river he placed a dot to mark Shangri-la Falls. "Now," said Gundersen, "if you follow the tip of my stick—"

"What are those marks on the ground?" asked Srin'gahar.

A map of your planet, Gundersen wanted to say. But there was no nildororu word in his mind for "map." He found that he also lacked words for "image," picture," and similar concepts. He said lamely, "This is your world. This is Belzagor, or at least half of it. See, this is the ocean, and the sun rises here, and—"

"How can this be my world, these marks, when my world is so large?"

"This is *like* your world. Each of these lines, here, stands for a place on your world. You see, here, the big river that runs out of the mist country and comes down to the coast, where the hotel is, yes? And this mark is the spaceport. These two lines are the top and the bottom of the northern mist country. The—"

"It takes a strong sulidor a march of many days to cross the northern mist country. said Srin'gahar. "I do not understand how you can point to such a small space and tell me it is the northern mist country. Forgive me, friend of my journey. I am very stupid."

Gundersen tried again, attempting to communicate the nature of the marks on the ground. But Srin'gahar simply could not comprehend the idea of a map, nor could he see how scratched lines could represent places. Gundersen considered asking Vol'himyor to help him, but rejected that plan when he realized that Vol'himyor, too, might not understand; it would be tactless to expose the many-born one's ignorance in any area. The map was a metaphor of place, an abstraction from reality. Evidently even beings possessing *g'rakh* might not have the capacity to grasp such abstractions.

He apologized to Srin'gahar for his own inability to express concepts clearly, and rubbed out the map with his boot. Without it, planning the route was somewhat more difficult, but they found ways to communicate. Gundersen learned that the great river at whose mouth the hotel was situated was called the Seran'nee in nildororu, and that the place where the river plunged out of the mountains into the coastal plain, which Earthmen knew as Shangri-la Falls, was Du'jayukh to nildoror. Then it was simple for them to agree to follow the Seran'nee to its source, with a stop at Du'jayukh and at any other settlement of Earthmen that happened to lie conveniently on the path north.

While this was being decided, several of the sulidoror brought a late breakfast of fruit and lake fish to Gundersen, exactly as though they recognized his authority under the Company. It was a curiously anachronistic gesture, almost servile, not at all like the way in which they had tossed him a raw slab of malidar meat the day before. Then they had been testing him, even taunting him; now they were waiting upon him. He was uncomfortable about that, but he was also quite hungry, and he made a point of asking Srin'gahar to tell him the sulidororu words of thanks. There was no sign that the powerful bipeds were pleased or flattered or amused by his use of their language, though.

They began their journey in late afternoon. The five nildoror moved in single file, Srin'gahar at the back of the group with Gundersen perched on his back; the Earthman did not appear to be the slightest burden for him. Their path led due north along the rim of the great rift, with the mountains that guarded the central plateau rising on their left. By the light of the sinking sun Gundersen stared toward that plateau. Down here in the valley, his surroundings had a certain familiarity; making the necessary allowances for the native plants and animals, he might almost be in some steamy jungle of South America. But the plateau appeared truly alien. Gundersen eyed the thick tangles of spiky purplish moss that festooned and nearly choked the trees along the top of the rift wall. The way the parasitic growth drowned its hosts the trees seemed grisly to him. The wall itself, of some soapy gray-green rock, dotted with angry blotches of crimson lichen and punctuated every few hundred meters by long ropy strands of a swollen blue fungus, cried out its otherworldliness: the soft mineral had never felt the impact of raindrops, but had been gently carved and shaped by the humidity alone, taking on weird knobbinesses and hollows over the millennia. Nowhere on Earth could one see a rock wall like that, serpentine and involute and greasy.

The forest beyond the wall looked impenetrable and vaguely sinister. The silence, the heavy and sluggish air, the sense of dark strangeness, the flexible limbs of the glossy trees bowed almost to the ground by moss, the occasional distant snort of some giant beast, made the central plateau seem forbidding and hostile. Few Earthmen had ever entered it, and it had never been surveyed in detail. The Company once had had some plans for stripping away large patches of jungle up there and putting in agricultural settlements, but nothing had come of the scheme, because of relinquishment. Gundersen had been in the plateau country only once, by accident, when his pilot had had to make a forced landing en route from coastal headquarters to the Sea of Dust. Seena had been with him. They spent a night and a day in that forest, Seena terrified from the moment of landing, Gundersen comforting her in a standard manly way but finding that her terror was somehow contagious. The girl trembled as one alien happening after another presented itself, and shortly Gundersen was on the verge of trembling too. They watched, fascinated and repelled, while an army of innumerable insects with iridescent hexagonal bodies and long hairy legs strode with maniacal persistence into a sprawling glade of tiger-moss; for hours the savage mouths of the carnivorous plants bit the shining insects into pieces and devoured them, and still the horde marched on to destruction. At last the moss was so glutted that it went into sporulation, puffing up cancerously and sending milky clouds of reproductive bodies spewing into the air. By morning the whole field of moss lay deflated and helpless, and tiny green reptiles with broad rasping tongues moved in to devour every strand, laying bare the soil for a new generation of flora. And then there were the feathery jelly-like things, streaked with blue and red, that hung in billowing cascades from the tallest trees, trapping unwary flying creatures. And bulky rough-skinned beasts as big as rhinos, bearing mazes of blue antlers with interlocking tines, grubbed for roots a dozen meters from their camp, glaring sourly at the strangers from Earth. And long-necked browsers with eyes like beacons munched on high leaves, squirting barrelfuls of purple urine from openings at the bases of their taut throats. And dark fat otter-like beings ran chattering past the stranded Earthmen, stealing anything within quick grasp. Other animals visited them also. This planet, which had never known the hunter's hand, abounded in big mammals. He and Seena and the pilot had seen more grotesqueness in a day and a night than they had bargained for when they signed up for outworld service.

"Have you ever been in there?" Gundersen asked Srin'gahar, as night began to conceal the rift wall.

"Never. My people seldom enter that land."

"Occasionally, flying low over the plateau, I used to see nildoror encampments in it. Not often, but sometimes. Do you mean that your people no longer go there?"

"No," said Srin'gahar. "A few of us have need to go to the plateau, but most do not. Sometimes the soul grows stale, and one must change one's surroundings. If one is not ready for rebirth, one goes to the plateau. It is easier to confront one's own soul in there, and to examine it for flaws. Can you understand what I say?"

"I think so," Gundersen said. "It's like a place of pilgrimage, then—a place of purification?"

"In a way."

"But why have the nildoror never settled permanently up there? There's plenty of food—the climate is warm—"

"It is not a place where *g'rakh* rules" the nildor replied.

"Is it dangerous to nildoror? Wild animals, poisonous plants, anything like that?"

"No, I would not say that. We have no fear of the plateau, and there is no place on this world that is dangerous to us. But the plateau does not interest us, except those who have the special need of which I spoke. As I say, *g'rakh* is foreign to it. Why should we go there? There is room enough for us in the lowlands."

The plateau is too alien even for them, Gundersen thought. They prefer their nice little jungle. How curious!

He was not sorry when darkness hid the plateau from view.

They made camp that night beside a hissing-hot stream. Evidently its waters issued from one of the underground cauldrons that were common in this sector of the continent; Srin'gahar said that the source lay not far to the north. Clouds of steam rose from the swift flow; the water, pink with high-temperature microorganisms, bubbled and boiled. Gundersen wondered if Srin'gahar had chosen this stopping place especially for his benefit, since nildoror had no use for hot water, but Earthmen notoriously did.

He scrubbed his face, taking extraordinary pleasure in it, and supplemented a dinner of food capsules and fresh fruit with a stew of greenberry roots—delectable when boiled, poisonous otherwise. For shelter while sleeping Gundersen used a monomolecular jungle blanket that he had stowed in his backpack, his one meager article of luggage on this journey. He draped the blanket over a tripod of boughs to keep away nightflies and other noxious insects, and crawled under it. The ground, thickly grassed, was a good enough mattress for him.

The nildoror did not seem disposed toward conversation. They left him alone. All but Srin'gahar moved several hundred meters upstream for the night. Srin'gahar settled down protectively a short distance from Gundersen and wished him a good sleep.

Gundersen said, "Do you mind talking a while? I want to know something about the process of rebirth. How do you know, for instance, that your time is upon you? Is it something you feel within yourself, or is it just a matter of reaching a certain age? Do you—" He became aware that Srin'gahar was paying no attention. The nildor had fallen into what might have been a deep trance, and lay perfectly still.

Shrugging, Gundersen rolled over and waited for sleep, but sleep was a long time coming.

He thought a good deal about the terms under which he had been permitted to make this northward journey. Perhaps another many-born one would have allowed him to go into the mist country without attaching the condition that he bring back Cedric Cullen; perhaps he would not have been granted safe-conduct at all. Gundersen suspected that the results would have been the same no matter which encampment of nildoror he had happened to go to for his travel permission. Though the nildoror had no means of long-distance communication, no governmental structure in an Earthly sense, no more coherence as a race than a population of jungle beasts, they nevertheless were remarkably well able to keep in touch with one another and to strike common policies.

What was it that Cullen had done, Gundersen wondered, to make him so eagerly sought?

In the old days Cullen had seemed overwhelmingly normal: a cheerful, amiable ruddy man who collected insects, spoke no harsh words, and held his liquor well. When Gundersen had been the chief agent out at Fire Point, in the Sea of Dust, a dozen years before, Cullen had been his assistant. Months on end there were only the two of them in the place, and Gundersen had come to know him quite well, he imagined. Cullen had no plans for making a career with the Company; he said he had signed a six-year contract, would not renew, and intended to take up a university appointment when he had done his time on Holman's World. He was here only for seasoning, and for the prestige that accrues to anyone who has a record of outworld service. But then the political situation of Earth grew complex, and the Company was forced to agree to relinquish a great many planets that it had colonized. Gundersen, like most of the fifteen thousand Company people here, had accepted a transfer to another assignment. Cullen, to Gundersen's amazement, was among the handful who opted to stay, even though that meant severing his ties with the home world. Gundersen had not asked him why; one did not discuss such things. But it seemed odd.

He saw Cullen clearly in memory, chasing bugs through the Sea of Dust, killing bottle jouncing against his hip as he ran from one rock outcropping to the next—an overgrown boy, really. The beauty of the Sea of Dust was altogether lost on him. No sector of the planet was more truly alien, nor more spectacular: a dry ocean bed, greater in size than the Atlantic, coated with a thick layer of fine crystalline mineral fragments as bright as mirrors when the sun was on them. From the station at Fire Point one could see the morning light advancing out of the east like a river of flame, spilling forth until the whole desert blazed. The crystals swallowed energy all day, and gave it forth all night, so that even at twilight the eerie radiance rose brightly, and after dark a throbbing purplish glow lingered for hours. In this almost lifeless but wondrously beautiful desert the Company had mined a dozen precious metals and thirty precious and semiprecious stones. The mining machines set forth from the station on far-ranging rounds, grinding up loveliness and returning with treasure; there was not much for an agent to do there except keep inventory of the mounting wealth and play host to the tourist parties that came to see the splendor of the countryside. Gundersen had grown terribly bored, and even the glories of the scenery had become tiresome to him; but Cullen, to whom the incandescent desert was merely a flashy nuisance, fell back on his hobby for entertainment, and filled bottle after bottle with his insects. Were the mining machines still standing in the Sea of Dust, Gundersen wondered, waiting for the command to resume operations? If the Company had not taken them away after relinquishment, they would surely stand there throughout all eternity, unrusting, useless, amidst the hideous gouges they had cut. The machines had scooped down through the crystalline layer to the dull basalt below, and had spewed out vast heaps of tailings and debris as they gnawed for wealth. Probably the Company had left the things behind, too, as monuments to commerce. Machinery was cheap, interstellar transport was costly; why bother removing them? "In another thousand years," Gundersen once had said, "the Sea of Dust will all be destroyed and there'll be nothing but rubble here, if these machines continue to chew up the rock at the present rate.'' Cullen had shrugged and smiled. ''Well, one won't need to wear these dark glasses, then, once the infernal glare is gone,'' he had said. ''Eh?'' And now the rape of the desert was over and the machines were still; and now Cullen was a fugitive in the mist country, wanted for some crime so terrible the nildoror would not even give it a name.

Seven

WHEN THEY TOOK to the road in the morning it was Srin'gahar, uncharacteristically, who opened the conversation.

"Tell me of elephants, friend of my journey. What do they look like, and how do they live?"

"Where did you hear of elephants?"

"The Earthpeople at the hotel spoke of them. And also in the past, I have heard the word said. They are beings of Earth that look like nildoror, are they not?"

"There is a certain resemblance," Gundersen conceded.

"A close one?"

"There are many similarities." He wished Srin'gahar were able to comprehend a sketch. "They are long and high in the body, like you, and they have four legs, and tails, and trunks. They have tusks, but only two, one here, one here. Their eyes are smaller and placed in a poor position, here, here. And here—" He indicated Srin'gahar's skullcrest. "Here they have nothing. Also their bones do not move as your bones do."

"It sounds to me," said Srin'gahar, "as though these elephants look very much like nildoror."

"I suppose they do."

"Why is this, can you say? Do you believe that we and the elephants can be of the same race?"

"It isn't possible," said Gundersen. "It's simply a—a—"

He groped for words; the nildororu vocabulary did not include the technical terms of genetics. "Simply a pattern in the development of life that occurs on many worlds. Certain basic designs of living creatures recur everywhere. The elephant design—the nildoror design—is one of them. The large body, the huge head, the short neck, the long trunk enabling the being to pick up objects and handle them without having to bend—these things will develop wherever the proper conditions are found."

"You have seen elephants, then, on many other worlds?"

"On some," Gundersen said. "Following the same general pattern of construction, or at least some aspects of it, although the closest resemblance of all is between elephants and nildoror. I could tell you of half a dozen other creatures that seem to belong to the same group. And this is also true of many other life-forms—insects, reptiles, small mammals, and so on. There are certain niches to be filled on every world. The thoughts of the Shaping Force travel the same path everywhere."

"Where, then, are Belzagor's equivalents of men?"

Gundersen faltered. "I didn't say that there were exact equivalents everywhere. The closest thing to the human pattern on your planet, I guess, is the sulidoror. And they aren't very close."

"On Earth, the men rule. Here the sulidoror are the secondary race."

"An accident of development. Your *g'rakh* is superior to that of the sulidoror; on our world we have no other species that possesses *g'rakh* at all. But the physical resemblances between men and sulidoror are many. They walk on two legs; so do we. They eat both flesh and fruit; so do we. They have hands which can grasp things; so do we. Their eyes are in front of their heads; so are ours. I know, they're bigger, stronger, hairier, and less intelligent than human beings, but I'm trying to show you how patterns can be similar on different planets, even though there's no real blood relationship between—"

Srin'gahar said quietly. "How do you know that elephants are without *g'rakh?*"

"We—they—it's clear that—" Gundersen stopped, uneasy. After a pause for thought he said carefully, "They've never demonstrated any of the qualities of *g'rakh*. They have no village life, no tribal structure, no technology, no religion, no continuing culture."

"We have no village life and no technology," the nildor said. "We wander through the jungles, stuffing ourselves with leaves and branches. I have heard this said of us, and it is true."

"But you're different. You—"

"How are we different? Elephants also wander through jungles, stuffing themselves with leaves and branches, do they not? They wear no skins over their own skins. They make no machines. They have no books. Yet you admit that we have *g'rakh*, and you insist that they do not."

"They can't communicate ideas," said Gundersen desperately. "They can tell each other simple things, I guess, about food and mating and danger, but that's all. If they have a true language, we can't detect it. We're aware of only a few basic sounds."

"Perhaps their language is so complex that you are *unable* to detect it," Srin'gahar suggested.

"I doubt that. We were able to tell as soon as we got here that the nildoror speak a language; and we were able to learn it. But in all the thousands of years that men and elephants have been sharing the same planet, we've never been able to see a sign that they can accumulate and transmit abstract concepts. And that's the essence of having *g'rakh,* isn't it?"

"I repeat my statement. What if you are so inferior to your elephants that you cannot comprehend their true depths?"

"A cleverly put point, Srin'gahar. But I won't accept it as any sort of description of the real world. If elephants have *g'rakh*, why haven't they managed to get anywhere in their whole time on Earth? Why does mankind dominate the planet, with the elephants crowded into a couple of small corners and practically wiped out?"

"You kill your elephants?"

"Not any more. But there was a time when men killed elephants for pleasure, or for food, or to use their tusks for ornaments. And there was a time when men used elephants for beasts of burden. If the elephants had *g'rakh*, they—"

He realized that he had fallen into Srin'gahar's trap.

The nildor said, "On this planet, too, the 'elephants' let themselves be exploited by mankind. You did not eat us and you rarely killed us, but often you made us work for you. And yet you admit we are beings of *g'rakh.*"

"What we did here," said Gundersen, "was a gigantic mistake, and when we came to realize it, we relinquished your world and got off it. But that still doesn't mean that elephants are rational and sentient beings. They're animals, Srin'gahar, big simple animals, and nothing more."

"Cities and machines are not the only achievements of *g'rakh.*"

"Where are their spiritual achievements, then? What does an elephant believe about the nature of the universe? What does he think about the Shaping Force? How does he regard his own place in his society?"

"I do not know," said Srin'gahar. "And neither do you, friend of my journey, because the language of the elephants is closed to you. But it is an error to assume the absence of *g'rakh* where you are incapable of seeing it."

"In that case, maybe the malidaror have *g'rakh* too. And the venom-serpents. And the trees, and the vines, and—"

"No," said Srin'gahar. "On this planet, only nildoror and sulidoror possess *g'rakh*. This we know beyond doubt. On your world it is not necessarily the case that humans alone have the quality of reason."

Gundersen saw the futility of pursuing the point. Was Srin'gahar a chauvinist defending the spiritual supremacy of elephants throughout the universe, or was he deliberately adopting an extreme position to expose the arrogances and moral vulnerabilities of Earth's imperialism? Gundersen did not know, but it hardly mattered. He thought of Gulliver discussing the intelligence of horses with the Houyhnhnms.

"I yield the point," he said curtly. "Perhaps someday I'll bring an elephant to Belzagor, and let you tell me whether or not it has *g'rakh.*"

"I would greet it as a brother."

"You might be unhappy over the emptiness of your brother's mind," Gundersen said. "You would see a being fashioned in your shape, but you wouldn't succeed in reaching its soul."

"Bring me an elephant, friend of my journey, and I will be the judge of its emptiness," said Srin'gahar. "But tell me one last thing, and then I will not trouble you: when your people call us elephants, it is because they think of us as mere beasts, yes? Elephants are 'big simple animals,' those are your words. Is this how the visitors from Earth see us?"

"They're referring only to the resemblance in form between nildoror and elephants. It's a superficial thing. They say you are *like* elephants."

"I wish I could believe that," the nildor said, and fell silent, leaving Gundersen alone with his shame and guilt. In the old days it had never been his habit to argue the nature of intelligence with his mounts. It had not even occurred to him then that such a debate might be possible. Now he sensed the extent of Srin'gahar's suppressed resentment. Elephants—yes, that was how he too had seen the nildoror. Intelligent elephants, perhaps. But still elephants.

In silence they followed the boiling stream northward. Shortly before noon they came to its source, a broad bow-shaped lake pinched between a double chain of steeply rising hills. Clouds of oily steam rose from the lake's surface. Thermophilic algae streaked its waters, the pink ones forming a thin scum on top and nearly screening the meshed tangles of the larger, thicker blue-gray plants a short distance underneath.

Gundersen felt some interest in stopping to examine the lake and its unusual life-forms. But he was strangely reluctant to ask Srin'gahar to halt. Srin'gahar was not only his carrier, he was his companion on a journey; and to say, tourist-fashion, "Let's stop here a while," might reinforce the nildor's belief that Earthmen still thought of his people merely as beasts of burden. So he resigned himself to passing up this bit of sightseeing. It was not right, he told himself, that he should delay Srin'gahar's journey toward rebirth merely to gratify a whim of idle curiosity.

But as they were nearing the lake's farther curve, there came such a crashing and smashing in the underbrush to the east that the entire procession of nildoror paused to see what was going on. To Gundersen it sounded as if some prowling dinosaur were about to come lurching out of the jungle, some huge clumsy tyrannosaur inexplicably displaced in time and space. Then, emerging from a break in the row of hills, there came slowly across the bare soil flanking the lake a little snub-snouted vehicle, which Gundersen recognized as the hotel's beetle, towing a crazy primitive-looking appendage of a trailer, fashioned from raw planks and large wheels. Atop this jouncing, clattering trailer four small tents had been pitched, covering most of its area; alongside the tents, over the wheels, luggage was mounted in several racks; and at the rear, clinging to a railing and peering nervously about, were the eight tourists whom Gundersen had last seen some days earlier in the hotel by the coast.

Srin'gahar said, "Here are some of your people. You will want to talk with them."

The tourists were, in fact, the last species whatever that Gundersen wanted to see at this point. He would have preferred locusts, scorpions, fanged serpents, tyrannosaurs, toads, anything at all. Here he was coming from some sort of mystical experience among the nildoror, the nature of which he barely understood; here, insulated from his own kind, he rode toward the land of rebirth struggling with basic questions of right and wrong, of the nature of intelligence, of the relationship of human to nonhuman and of himself to his own past; only a few moments before he had been forced into an uncomfortable, even painful confrontation with that past by Srin'gahar's casual, artful questions about the souls of elephants; and abruptly Gundersen found himself once more among these empty, trivial human beings, these archetypes of the ignorant and blind tourist, and whatever individuality he had earned in the eyes of his nildor companion vanished instantly as he dropped back into the undifferentiated class of Earthmen. These tourists, some part of his mind knew, were not nearly as vulgar and hollow as he saw them; they were merely ordinary people, friendly, a bit foolish, overprivileged, probably quite satisfactory human beings within the context of their lives on Earth, and only seeming to be cardboard figurines here because they were essentially irrelevant to the planet they had chosen to visit. But he was not yet ready to have Srin'gahar lose sight of him as a person separate from all the other Earthmen who came to Belzagor, and he feared that the tide of bland chatter welling out of these people would engulf him and make him one of them.

The beetle, obviously straining to haul the trailer, came to rest a dozen meters from the edge of the lake. Out of it came Van Beneker, looking sweatier and seedier than usual. ''All right,'' he called to the tourists. ''Everyone down! We're going to have a look at one of the famous hot lakes!'' Gundersen, high atop Srin'gahar's broad back, considered telling the nildor to move along. The other four nildoror, having satisfied themselves about the cause of the commotion, had already done that and were nearly out of view at the far end of the lake. But he decided to stay a while; he knew that a display of snobbery toward his own species would win him no credit with Srin'gahar.

Van Beneker turned to Gundersen and called out, ''Morning, sir! Glad to see you! Having a good trip?''

The four Earth couples clambered down from their trailer. They were fully in character, behaving exactly as Gundersen's harsh image of them would have them behave: they seemed bored and glazed, surfeited with the alien wonders they had already seen. Stein, the helix-parlor proprietor, dutifully checked the aperture of his camera, mounted it in his cap, and routinely took a 360-degree hologram of the scene; but when the printout emerged from the camera's output slot a moment later he did not even bother to glance at it. The act of picture-taking, not the picture itself, was significant. Watson, the doctor, muttered a joyless joke of some sort to Christopher, the financier, who responded with a mechanical chuckle. The women, bedraggled and jungle-stained, paid no attention to the lake. Two simply leaned against the beetle and waited to be told what it was they were being shown, while the other two, as they became aware of Gundersen's presence, pulled facial masks from their backpacks and hurriedly slipped the thin plastic films over their heads so that they could present at least the illusion of properly groomed features before the handsome stranger.

''I won't stay here long,'' Gundersen heard himself promising Srin'gahar, as he dismounted.

Van Beneker came up to him. ''What a trip!'' the little man

blurted. "What a stinking trip! Well, I ought to be used to it by now. How's everything been going for you, Mr. G?"

"No complaints." Gundersen nodded at the trailer. "Where'd you get that noisy contraption?"

"We built it a couple of years ago when one of the old cargo haulers broke down. Now we use it to take tourists around when we can't get any nildoror bearers."

"It looks like something out of the eighteenth century."

"Well, you know, sir, out here we don't have much left in the way of modern equipment. We're short of servos and hydraulic walkers and all that. But you can always find wheels and some planks around. We make do."

"What happened to the nildoror we were riding coming from the spaceport to the hotel? I thought they were willing to work for you."

"Sometimes yes, sometimes no," Van Beneker said. "They're unpredictable. We can't force them to work, and we can't hire them to work. We can only ask them politely, and if they say they're not available, that's it. Couple of days back, they decided they weren't going to be available for a while, so we had to get out the trailer." He lowered his voice. "If you ask me, it's on account of these eight baboons here. They think the nildoror don't understand any English, and they keep telling each other how terrible it is that we had to hand a planet as valuable as this over to a bunch of elephants."

"On the voyage out here," said Gundersen, "some of them were voicing quite strong liberal views. At least two of them were big pro-relinquishment people."

"Sure. Back on Earth they bought relinquishment as a political theory. 'Give the colonized worlds back to their long-oppressed natives,' and all that. Now they're out here and suddenly they've decided that the nildoror aren't 'natives,' just animals, just funny-looking elephants, and maybe we should have kept the place after all." Van Beneker spat. "And the nildoror take it all in. They pretend they don't understand the lauguage, but they do, they do. You think they feel like hauling people like that on their backs?"

"I see," said Gundersen. He glanced at the tourists. They were eyeing Srin'gahar, who had wandered off toward the bush and was energetically ripping soft boughs loose for his midday meal. Watson nudged Miraflores, who quirked his lips and shook his head as if in disapproval. Gundersen could not hear what they were saying, but he imagined that they were expressing scorn for Srin'gahar's enthusiastic foraging. Evidently civilized beings were not supposed to pull their meals off trees with their trunks.

Van Beneker said, "You'll stay and have lunch with us, won't you, Mr. G?"

"That's very kind of you," Gundersen said.

He squatted in the shade while Van Beneker rounded up his charges and led them down to the rim of the steaming lake. When they were all there Gundersen rose and quietly affiliated himself with the group. He listened to the guide's spiel, but managed to train only half his attention on what was being said. "High-temperature life-zone . . . better than 70°C . . . more in some places, even above boiling, yet things live in it . . . special genetic adaptation . . . thermophilic, we call it, that is, heat-loving . . . the DNA doesn't get cooked, no, but the rate of spontaneous mutation is pretty damned high, and the species change so fast you wouldn't believe it . . . enzymes resist the heat . . . put the lake organisms in cool water and they'll freeze in about a minute . . . life processes extraordinarily fast . . . unfolded and denatured proteins can also function when circumstances are such that . . . you get quite a range up to middle-phylum level . . . a pocket environment, no interaction with the rest of the planet . . . thermal gradients . . . quantitative studies . . . the famous kinetic biologist, Dr. Brock . . . continuous thermal destruction of sensitive molecules . . . unending resynthesis. . . ."

Srin'gahar was still stuffing himself with branches. It seemed to Gundersen that he was eating far more than he normally did at this time of day. The sounds of rending and chewing clashed with the jerky drone of Van Beneker's memorized scientific patter.

Now, unhooking a biosensitive net from his belt, Van Beneker began to dredge up samples of the lake's fauna for the edification of his group. He gripped the net's handle and made vernier adjustments governing the mass and length of the desired prey; the net, mounted at the end of an almost infinitely expandable length of fine flexible metal coil, swept back and forth beneath the surface of the lake, hunting for organisms of the programmed dimensions. When its sensors told it that it was in the presence of living matter, its mouth snapped open and quickly shut again. Van Beneker retracted it, bringing to shore some unhappy prisoner trapped within a sample of its own scalding environment.

Out came one lake creature after another, red-skinned, boiled-looking, but live and angry and flapping. An armored fish emerged, concealed in shining plates, embellished with fantastic excrescences and ornaments. A lobster-like thing came forth, lashing a long spiked tail, waving ferocious eye-stalks. Up from the lake came something that was a single immense claw with a tiny vestigial body. No two of Van Beneker's grotesque catches were alike. The heat of the lake, he repeated, induces frequent mutations. He rattled off the whole genetic explanation a second time, while dumping one little monster back into the hot bath and probing for the next.

The genetic aspects of the thermophilic creatures seemed to catch the interest of only one of the tourists—Stein, who, as a helix-parlor owner specializing in the cosmetic editing of human genes, would know more than a little about mutation himself. He asked a few intelligent-sounding questions, which Van Beneker naturally was unable to answer; the others simply stared, patiently waiting for their guide to finish showing them funny animals and take them somewhere else. Gundersen, who had never had a chance before to examine the contents of one of these high-temperature pockets, was grateful for the exhibition, although the sight of writhing captive lake-dwellers quickly palled on him. He became eager to move on.

He glanced around and discovered that Srin'gahar was nowhere in sight.

"What we've got this time," Van Beneker was saying, "is the most dangerous animal of the lake, what we call a razor shark. Only I've never seen one like this before. You see those little horns? Absolutely new. And that lantern sort of thing on top of the head, blinking on and off?" Squirming in the net was a slender crimson creature about a meter in length. Its entire underbelly, from snout to gut, was hinged, forming what amounted to one gigantic mouth rimmed by hundreds of needle-like teeth. As the mouth opened and closed, it seemed as if the whole animal were splitting apart and healing itself. "This beast feeds on anything up to three times its own size," Van Beneker said. "As you can see, it's fierce and savage, and—"

Uneasy, Gundersen drifted away from the lake to look for Srin'gahar. He found the place where the nildor had been eating, where the lower branches of several trees were stripped bare. He saw what seemed to be the nildor's trail, leading away into the jungle. A painful white light of desolation flared in his skull at the awareness that Srin'gahar must quietly have abandoned him.

In that case his journey would have to be interrupted. He did not dare go alone and on foot into that pathless wilderness ahead. He would have to ask Van Beneker to take him back to some nildoror encampment where he might find another means of getting to the mist country.

The tour group was coming up from the lake now. Van Beneker's net was slung over his shoulder; Gundersen saw some lake creatures moving slowly about in it.

"Lunch," he said. "I got us some jelly-crabs. You hungry?"

Gundersen managed a thin smile. He watched, not at all hungry, as Van Beneker opened the net; a gush of hot water rushed from it, carrying along eight or ten oval purplish creatures, each different from the others in the number of legs, shell markings, and size of claws. They crawled in stumbling circles, obviously annoyed by the relative coolness of the air. Steam rose from their backs. Expertly Van Beneker pithed them with sharpened sticks, and cooked them with his fusion torch, and split open their shells to reveal the pale quivering jelly-like metabolic regulators within. Three of the woman grimaced and turned away, but Mrs. Miraflores took her crab and ate it with delight. The men seemed to enjoy it. Gundersen, merely nibbling at the jelly, eyed the forest and worried about Srin'gahar.

Scraps of conversation drifted toward him.

"—enormous profit potential, just wasted, altogether

wasted—"

"—even so, our obligation is to encourage self-determination on every planet that—"

"—but are they *people*?"

"—look for the soul, it's the only way to tell that—"

"—elephants, and nothing but elephants. Did you see him ripping up the trees and—"

"—relinquishment was the fault of a highly vocal minority of bleeding hearts who—"

"—no soul, no relinquishment—"

"—you're being too harsh, dear. There were definite abuses on some of the planets, and—"

"—stupid political expediency, I call it. The blind leading the blind—"

"—can they write? Can they think? Even in Africa we were dealing with human beings, and even there—"

"—the soul, the inner spirit—"

"—I don't need to tell you how much I favored relinquishment. You remember, I took the petitions around and everything. But even so, I have to admit that after seeing—"

"—piles of purple crap on the beach—"

"—victims of sentimental overreaction—"

"—I understand the annual profit was on the order of—"

"—no doubt that they have souls. No doubt at all." Gundersen realized that his own voice had entered the conversation. The others turned to him; there was a sudden vacuum to fill. He said, "They have a religion, and that implies the awareness of the existence of a spirit, a soul, doesn't it?"

"What kind of religion?" Miraflores asked.

"I'm not sure. One important part of it is ecstatic dancing—a kind of frenzied prancing around that leads to some sort of mystic experience. I know. I've danced with them. I've felt at least the edges of that experience. And they've got a thing called rebirth, which I suppose is central to their rituals. I don't understand it. They go north, into the mist country, and something happens to them there. They've always kept the details a secret. I think the sulidoror give them something, some drug, maybe, and it rejuvenates them in some inner way, and leads to a kind of illumination—am I at all clear?'' Gundersen, as he spoke, was working his way almost unconsciously through the pile of uneaten jelly-crabs. ''All I can tell you is that rebirth is vitally important to them, and they seem to derive their tribal status from the number of rebirths they've undergone. So you see they're not just animals. They have a society, they have a cultural structure—complex, difficult for us to grasp.''

Watson asked, ''Why don't they have a civilization, then?''

''I've just told you that they do.''

''I mean cities, machines, books—''

''They're not physically equipped for writing, for building things, for any small manipulations,'' Gundersen said. ''Don't you see, they have no *hands?* A race with hands makes one kind of society. A race built like elephants makes another.'' He was drenched in sweat and his appetite was suddenly insatiable. The women, he noticed, were staring at him strangely. He realized why: he was cleaning up all the food in sight, compulsively stuffing it into his mouth. Abruptly his patience shattered and he felt that his skull would explode if he did not instantly drop all barriers and admit the one great guilt that by stabbing his soul had spurred him into strange odysseys. It did not matter that these were not the right people from whom to seek absolution. The words rushed uncontrollably upward to his lips and he said, ''When I came here I was just like you. I underestimated the nildoror. Which led me into a grievous sin that I have to explain to you. You know, I was a sector administrator for a while, and one of my jobs was arranging the efficient deployment of native labor. Since we didn't fully understand that the nildoror were intelligent autonomous beings, we *used* them, we put them to work on heavy construction jobs, lifting girders with their trunks, anything we thought they were capable of handling on sheer muscle alone. We just ordered them around as if they were machines.'' Gundersen closed his eyes and felt the past roaring toward him, inexorably, a black cloud of memory that enveloped and overwhelmed him, ''The nildoror let us use them, God knows why. I guess we were the crucible in which their race had to be purged. Well, one day a dam broke, out in Monroe District up in the north, not far from where the mist country begins, and a whole thornbush plantation was in danger of flooding, at a loss to the Company of who knows how many millions. And the main power plant of the district was endangered too, along with our station headquarters and—let's just say that if we didn't react fast, we'd lose our entire investment in the north. My responsibility. I began conscripting nildoror to build a secondary line of dikes. We threw every robot we had into the job, but we didn't have enough, so we got the nildoror too, long lines of them plodding in from every part of the jungle, and we worked day and night until we were all ready to fall down dead. We were beating the flood, but I couldn't be sure of it. And on the sixth morning I drove out to the dike site to see if the next crest would break through, and there were seven nildoror I hadn't ever seen before, marching along a path going north. I told them to follow me. They refused, very gently. They said, no, they were on their way to the mist country for the rebirth ceremony, and they couldn't stop. Rebirth? What did I care about rebirth? I wasn't going to take that excuse from them, not when it looked like I might lose my whole district. Without thinking I ordered them to report for dike duty or I'd execute them on the spot. Rebirth can wait, I said. Get reborn some other time. This is serious business. They put their heads down and pushed the tips of their tusks into the ground. That's a sign of great sadness among them. Their spines drooped. Sad. Sad. We pity you, one of them said to me, and I got angry and told him what he could do with his pity. Where did he get the right to pity me? Then I pulled my fusion torch. Go on, get moving, there's a work crew that needs you. Sad. Big eyes looking pity at me. Tusks in the ground. Two or three of the nildoror said they were very sorry, they couldn't do any work for me now, it was impossible for them to break their journey. But they were ready to die right there, if I insisted on it. They didn't want to hurt my prestige by defying me, but they *had* to defy me, and so they were willing to pay the price. I was about to fry one, as an example to the others, and then I stopped and said to myself, what the hell am I doing, and the nildoror waited, and my aides were watching and so were some of our other nildoror, and I lifted the fusion torch again, telling myself that I'd kill one of them, the one who said he pitied me, and hoping that then the others would come to their senses. They just waited. Calling my bluff. How could I fry seven pilgrims even if they were defying a sector chief's direct order? But my authority was at stake. So I pushed the trigger. I just gave him a slow burn, not deep, enough to scar the hide, that was all, but the nildor stood there taking it, and in another few minutes I would have burned right through to a vital organ. And so I soiled myself in front of them by using force. It was what they had been waiting for. Then a couple of the nildoror who looked older than the others said, Stop it, we wish to reconsider, and I turned off the torch, and they went aside for a conference. The one I had burned was hobbling a little, and looked hurt, but he wasn't badly wounded, not nearly as badly as I was. The one who pushes the trigger can get hurt worse than his target, do you know that? And in the end the nildoror all agreed to do as I asked. So instead of going north for rebirth they went to work on the dike, even the burned one, and nine days later the flood crest subsided and the plantation and the power plant and all the rest were saved and we lived happily ever after.'' Gundersen's voice trailed off. He had made his confession, and now he could not face these people any longer. He picked up the shell of the one remaining crab and explored it for some scrap of jelly, feeling depleted and drained. There was an endless span of silence.

Then Mrs. Christopher said, ''So what happened then?''

Gundersen looked up, blinking. He thought he had told it all.

''Nothing happened then,'' he said. ''The flood crest subsided.''

''But what was the point of the story?''

He wanted to hurl the empty crab in her tensely smiling face. ''The point?'' he said. ''The point? Why— '' He was dizzy, now. He said, ''Seven intelligent beings were journeying toward the holiest rite of their religion, and at gunpoint I requisitioned their services on a construction job to save property that meant nothing to them, and they came and hauled logs for me. Isn't the point obvious enough? Who was spiritually superior there? When you treat a rational autonomous creature as though he's a mere beast, what does that make you?''

''But it was an emergency,'' said Watson. ''You needed all the help you could get. Surely other considerations could be laid aside at a time like that. So they were nine days late getting to their rebirth. Is that so bad?''

Gundersen said hollowly, ''A nildor goes to rebirth only when the time is ripe, and I can't tell you how they know the time is ripe, but perhaps it's astrological, something to do with the conjunction of the moons. A nildor has to get to the place of rebirth at the propitious time, and if he doesn't make it in time, he isn't reborn just then. Those seven nildoror were already late, because the heavy rains had washed out the roads in the south. The nine days more that I tacked on made them *too* late. When they were finished building dikes for me, they simply went back south to rejoin their tribe. I didn't understand why. It wasn't until much later that I found out that I had cost them their chance at rebirth and they might have to wait ten or twenty years until they could go again. Or maybe never get another chance.'' Gundersen did not feel like talking any more. His throat was dry. His temples throbbed. How cleansing it would be, he thought, to dive into the steaming lake. He got stiffly to his feet, and as he did so he noticed that Srin'gahar had returned and was standing motionless a few hundred meters away, beneath a mighty swordflower tree.

He said to the tourists, ''The point is that the nildoror have religion and souls, and that they are people, and that if you can buy the concept of relinquishment at all, you can't object to relinquishing this planet. The point is also that when Earthmen collide with an alien species they usually do so with maximum misunderstanding. The point is furthermore that I'm not surprised you think of the nildoror the way you do, because I did too, and learned a little better when it was too late to matter, and even so I didn't learn enough to do me any real good, which is one of the reasons why I came back to this planet. And I'd like you to excuse me now, because this is the propitious time for me to move on, and I have to go.'' He walked quickly away from them.

Approaching Srin'gahar, he said, ''I'm ready to leave now.''

The nildor knelt. Gundersen remounted.

"Where did you go?" the Earthman asked. "I was worried when you disappeared."

"I felt that I should leave you alone with your friends," said Srin'gahar. "Why did you worry? There is an obligation on me to bring you safely to the country of the mist."

Eight

THE QUALITY OF the land was undoubtedly changing. They were leaving the heart of the equatorial jungle behind, and starting to enter the highlands that led into the mist zone. The climate here was still tropical, but the humidity was not so intense; the atmosphere, instead of holding everything in a constant clammy embrace, released its moisture periodically in rain, and after the rain the texture of the air was clear and light until its wetness was renewed. There was different vegetation in this region: harsh-looking angular stuff, with stiff leaves sharp as blades. Many of the trees had luminous foliage that cast a cold light over the forest by night. There were fewer vines here, and the treetops no longer formed a continuous canopy shutting out most of the sunlight; splashes of brightness dappled the forest floor, in some places extending across broad open plazas and meadows. The soil, leached by the frequent rains, was a pale yellowish hue, not the rich black of the jungle. Small animals frequently sped through the underbrush. At a slower pace moved solemn slug-like creatures, blue-green with ebony mantles, which Gundersen recognized as the mobile fungoids of the highlands—plants that crawled from place to place in quest of fallen boughs or a lightning-shattered tree-trunk. Both nildoror and men considered their taste a great delicacy.

On the evening of the third day northward from the place of the boiling lake Srin'gahar and Gundersen came upon the other four nildoror, who had marched on ahead. They were camped at the foot of a jagged crescent-shaped hill, and evidently had been there at least a day, judging by the destruction they had worked upon the foliage all around their resting-place. Their trunks and faces, smeared and stained with luminous juices, glowed brightly. With them was a sulidor, by far the largest one Gundersen had ever seen, almost twice Gundersen's own height, with a pendulous snout the length of a man's forearm. The sulidor stood erect beside a boulder encrusted with blue moss, his legs spread wide and his tail, tripod fashion, bracing his mighty weight. Narrowed eyes surveyed Gundersen from beneath shadowy hoods. His long arms, tipped with terrifying curved claws, hung at rest. The fur of the sulidor was the color of old bronze, and unusually thick.

One of the candidates for rebirth, a female nildor called Luu'khamin, said to Gundersen, "The sulidor's name is Na-sinisul. He wishes to speak with you."

"Let him speak, then."

"He prefers that you know, first, that he is not a sulidor of the ordinary kind. He is one of those who administers the ceremony of rebirth, and we will see him again when we approach the mist country. He is a sulidor of rank and merit, and his words are not to be taken lightly. Will you bear that in mind as you listen to him?"

"I will. I take no one's words lightly on this world, but I will give him a careful hearing beyond any doubt. Let him speak."

The sulidor strode a short distance forward and once again planted himself firmly, digging his great spurred feet deep into the resilient soil. When he spoke, it was in nildororu stamped with the accent of the north: thick-tongued, slow, positive.

"I have been on a journey," said Na-sinisul, "to the Sea of Dust, and now I am returning to my own land to aid in the preparations for the event of rebirth in which these five travelers are to take part. My presence here is purely accidental. Do you understand that I am not in this place for any particular purpose involving you or your companions?"

"I understand," said Gundersen, astounded by the precise

and emphatic manner of the sulidor's speech. He had known the sulidoror only as dark, savage, ferocious-looking figures lurking in mysterious glades.

Na-sinisul continued, "As I passed near here yesterday, I came by chance to the site of a former station of your Company. Again by chance, I chose to look within, though it was no business of mine to enter that place. Within I found two Earthmen whose bodies had ceased to serve them. They were unable to move and could barely talk. They requested me to send them from this world, but I could not do such a thing on my own authority. Therefore I ask you to follow me to this station and to give me instructions. My time is short here, so it must be done at once."

"How far is it?"

"We could be there before the rising of the third moon."

Gundersen said to Srin'gahar, "I don't remember a Company station here. There should be one a couple of days north of here, but—"

"This is the place where the food that crawls was collected and shipped downriver," said the nildor.

"Here?" Gundersen shrugged. "I guess I've lost my bearings again. All right, I'll go there." To Na-sinisul he said, "Lead and I'll follow."

The sulidor moved swiftly through the glowing forest, and Gundersen, atop Srin'gahar, rode just to his rear. They seemed to be descending, and the air grew warm and murky. The landscape also changed, for the trees here had aerial roots that looped up like immense scraggy elbows, and the fine tendrils sprouting from the roots emitted a harsh green radiance. The soil was loose and rocky; Gundersen could hear it crunching under Srin'gahar's tread. Bird-like things were perched on many of the roots. They were owlish creatures that appeared to lack all color; some were black, some white, some a mottled black and white. He could not tell if that was their true hue or if the luminosity of the vegetation simply robbed them of color. A sickly fragrance came from vast, pallid parasitic flowers sprouting from the trunks of the trees.

By an outcropping of naked, weathered yellow rock lay the remains of the Company station. It seemed even more thoroughly ruined than the serpent station far to the south; the dome of its roof had collapsed and coils of wiry-stemmed saprophytes were clinging to its sides, perhaps feeding on the decomposition products that the rain eroded from the abrasions in the plastic walls. Srin'gahar allowed Gundersen to dismount. The Earthman hesitated outside the building, waiting for the sulidor to take the lead. A fine warm rain began to fall; the tang of the forest changed at once, becoming sweet where it had been sour. But it was the sweetness of decay.

"The Earthmen are inside," said Na-sinisul. "You may go in. I await your instructions."

Gundersen entered the building. The reek of rot was far more intense here, concentrated, perhaps, by the curve of the shattered dome. The dampness was all-pervasive. He wondered what sort of virulent spores he sucked into his nostrils with every breath. Something dripped in the darkness, making a loud tocking sound against the lighter patter of the rain coming through the gaping roof. To give himself light, Gundersen drew his fusion torch and kindled it at the lowest beam. The warm white glow spread through the station. At once he felt a flapping about his face as some thermotropic creature, aroused and attracted by the heat of the torch, rose up toward it. Gundersen brushed it away; there was slime on his fingertips afterward.

Where were the Earthmen?

Cautiously he made a circuit of the building. He remembered it vaguely, now—one of the innumerable bush stations the Company once had scattered across Holman's World. The floor was split and warped, requiring him to climb over the buckled, sundered sections. The mobile fungoids crawled everywhere, devouring the scum that covered all interior surfaces of the building and leaving narrow glistening tracks behind. Gundersen had to step carefully to avoid putting his feet on the creatures, and he was not always successful. Now he came to a place where the building widened, puckering outward; he flashed his torch around and caught sight of a blackened wharf, overlooking the bank of a swift river. Yes, he remembered. The fungoids were wrapped and baled here and sent downriver on their voyage toward the market. But the Company's barges no longer stopped here, and the tasty pale slugs now wandered unmolested over the mossy relics of furniture and equipment.

"Hello?" Gundersen called. "Hello, hello, hello?"

He received a moan by way of answer. Stumbling and slipping in the dimness, fighting a swelling nausea, he forced his way onward through a maze of unseen obstacles. He came to the source of the loud dripping sound. Something bright red and basket-shaped and about the size of a man's chest had established itself high on the wall, perpendicular to the floor. Through large pores in its spongy surface a thick black fluid exuded, falling in a continuous greasy splash. As the light of Gundersen's torch probed it, the exudation increased, becoming almost a cataract of tallowy liquid. When he moved the light away the flow became less copious, though still heavy.

The floor sloped here so that whatever dripped from the spongy basket flowed quickly down, collecting at the far side of the room in the angle between the floor and the wall. Here Gundersen found the Earthmen. They lay side by side on a low mattress; fluid from the dripping thing had formed a dark pool around them, completely covering the mattress and welling up over the bodies. One of the Earthmen, head lolling to the side, had his face totally immersed in the stuff. From the other one came the moans.

They both were naked. One was a man, one a woman, though Gundersen had some difficulty telling that at first; both were so shrunken and emaciated that the sexual characteristics were obscured. They had no hair, not even eybrows. Bones protruded through parchment-like skin. The eyes of both were open, but were fixed in a rigid, seemingly sightless stare, unblinking, glassy. Lips were drawn back from teeth. Grayish algae sprouted in the furrows of their skins, and the mobile fungoids roamed their bodies, feeding on this growth. With a quick automatic gesture of revulsion Gundersen plucked two of the slug-like creatures from the woman's empty breasts. She stirred; she moaned again. In the language of the nildoror she murmured, "Is it over yet?" Her voice was like a flute played by a sullen desert breeze.

Speaking English, Gundersen said, "Who are you? How did this happen?"

He got no response from her. A fungoid crept across her mouth, and he flicked it aside. He touched her cheek. There was a rasping sound as his hand ran across her skin; it was like caressing stiff paper. Struggling to remember her, Gundersen imagined dark hair on her bare skull, gave her light arching brows, saw her cheeks full and her lips smiling. But nothing registered; either he had forgotten her, or he had never known her, or she was unrecognizable in her present condition.

"Is it over soon?" she asked, again in nildororu.

He turned to her companion. Gently, half afraid the fragile neck would snap, Gundersen lifted the man's head out of the pool of fluid. It appeared that he had been breathing it; it trickled from his nose and lips, and after a moment he showed signs of being unable to cope with ordinary air. Gundersen let his face slip back into the pool. In that brief moment he had recognized the man as a certain Harold—or was it Henry?—Dykstra, whom he had known distantly in the old days.

The unknown woman was trying to move one arm. She lacked the strength to lift it. These two were like living ghosts, like death-in-life, mired in their sticky fluid and totally helpless. In the language of the nildoror he said, "How long have you been this way?"

"Forever," she whispered.

"Who are you?"

"I don't... remember. I'm... waiting."

"For what?"

"For the end."

"Listen," he said, "I'm Edmund Gundersen, who used to be sector chief. I want to help you."

"Kill me first. Then him."

"We'll get you out of here and back to the spaceport. We can have you on the way to Earth in a week or ten days, and then—"

"No... please...."

"What's wrong?" he asked.

"Finish it. Finish it." She found enough strength to arch her back, lifting her body halfway out of the fluid that nearly concealed her lower half. Something rippled and briefly bulged beneath her skin. Gundersen touched the taut belly and felt movement within, and that quick inward quiver was the most frightening sensation he had ever known. He touched the body of Dykstra, too: it also rippled inwardly.

Appalled, Gundersen scrambled to his feet and backed away from them. By faint torchlight he studied their shriveled bodies, naked but sexless, bone and ligament, shorn of flesh and spirit yet still alive. A terrible fear came over him. "Na-sinisul!" he called. "Come in here! Come in!"

The sulidor was at his side. Gundersen said, "Something's inside their bodies. Some kind of parasite? It moves. What is it?"

"Look there," said Na-sinisul, indicating the spongy basket from which the dark fluid trickled. "They carry its young. They have become hosts. A year, two years, perhaps three, and the larvae will emerge."

"Why aren't they both dead?"

"They draw nourishment from this," said the sulidor, swishing his tail through the black flow. "It seeps into their skins. It feeds them, and it feeds that which is within them."

"If we took them out of here and sent them down to the hotel on rafts—?"

"They would die," Na-sinisul said, "moments after they were removed from the wetness about them. There is no hope of saving them."

"When does it end?" the woman asked.

Gundersen trembled. All his training told him never to accept the finality of death; any human in whom some shred of life remained could be saved, rebuilt from a few scraps of cells into a reasonable facsimile of the original. But there were no facilities for such things on this world. He confronted a swirl of choices. Leave them here to let alien things feed upon their guts; try to bring them back to the spaceport for shipment to the nearest tectogenetic hospital; put them out of their misery at once; seek to free their bodies himself of whatever held them in thrall. He knelt again. He forced himself to experience that inner quivering again. He touched the woman's stomach, her thighs, her bony haunches. Beneath the skin she was a mass of strangeness. Yet her mind still ticked, though she had forgotten her name and her native language. The man was luckier; though he was infested too, at least Dykstra did not have to lie here in the dark waiting for the death that could come only when the harbored larvae erupted from the enslaved human flesh. Was this what they had desired, when they refused repatriation from this world that they loved? An Earthman can become captured by Belzagor, the many-born nildor Vol'himyor had said. But this was too literal a capture.

The stink of bodily corruption made him retch.

"Kill them both," he said to Na-sinisul. "And be quick about it."

"This is what you instruct me to do?"

"Kill them. And rip down that thing on the wall and kill it too."

"It has given no offense," said the sulidor. "It has done only what is natural to its kind. By killing these two, I will deprive it of its young, but I am not willing to deprive it of life as well."

"All right," Gundersen said. "Just the Earthmen, then. Fast."

"I do this as an act of mercy, under your direct orders," said Na-sinisul. He leaned forward and lifted one powerful arm. The savage curved claws emerged fully from their sheath. The arm descended twice.

Gundersen compelled himself to watch. The bodies split like dried husks; the things within came spilling out, unformed, raw. Even now, in some inconceivable reflex, the two corpses twitched and jerked. Gundersen stared into their eroded depths. "Do you hear me?" he asked. "Are you alive or dead?" The woman's mouth gaped but no sound came forth, and he did not know whether this was an attempt to speak or merely a last convulsion of the ravaged nerves. He stepped his fusion torch up to high power and trained it on the dark pool. I am the resurrection and the life, he thought, reducing Dykstra to ashes, and the woman beside him, and the squirming unfinished larvae. Acrid, choking fumes rose; not even the torch could destroy the building's dampness. He turned the torch back to illumination level. "Come," he said to the sulidor, and they went out together.

"I feel like burning the entire building and purifying this

place," Gundersen said to Na-sinisul.

"I know."

"But you would prevent me."

"You are wrong. No one on this world will prevent you from doing anything."

But what good would it do, Gundersen asked himself. The purification had already been accomplished. He had removed the only beings in this place that were foreign to it.

The rain had stopped. To the waiting Srin'gahar, Gundersen said, "Will you take me away from here?"

They rejoined the other four nildoror. Then, because they had lingered too long here and the land of rebirth was still far away, they resumed the march, even though it was night. By morning Gundersen could hear the thunder of Shangri-la Falls, which the nildoror called Du'jayukh.

Nine

IT WAS AS though a white wall of water descended from the sky. Nothing on Earth could match the triple plunge of this cataract, by which Madden's River, or the Seran'nee, dropped five hundred meters, and then six hundred, and then five hundred more, falling from ledge to ledge in its tumble toward the sea. Gundersen and the five nildoror stood at the foot of the falls, where the entire violent cascade crashed into a broad rock-flanged basin out of which the serpentine river continued its southeasterly course; the sulidor had taken his leave in the night and was proceeding northward by his own route. To Gundersen's rear lay the coastal plain, behind his right shoulder, and the central plateau, behind his left. Before him, up by the head of the falls, the northern plateau began, the highlands that controlled the approach to the mist country. Just as a titanic north-south rift cut the coastal plain off from the central plateau, so did another rift running east-west separate both the central plateau and the coastal plain from the highlands ahead.

He bathed in a crystalline pool just beyond the tumult of the cataract, and then they began their ascent. The Shangri-la Station, one of the Company's most important outposts, was invisible from below; it was set back a short way from the head of the falls. Once there had been waystations at the foot of the falls and at the head of the middle cataract, but no trace of these structures remained; the jungle had swallowed them utterly in only eight years. A winding road, with an infinity of switchbacks, led to the top. When he first had seen it, Gundersen had imagined it was the work of Company engineers, but he had learned that it was a natural ridge in the face of the plateau, which the nildoror themselves had enlarged and deepened to make their journey toward rebirth more easy.

The swaying rhythm of his mount lulled him into a doze; he held tight to Srin'gahar's pommel-like horns and prayed that in his grogginess he would not fall off. Once he woke suddenly and found himself clinging only by his left hand, with his body half slung out over a sheer drop of at least two hundred meters. Another time, drowsy again, he felt cold spray and snapped to attention to see the entire cascade of the falling river rushing past him no more than a dozen meters away. At the head of the lowest cataract the nildoror paused to eat, and Gundersen dashed icy water in his face to shatter his sluggishness. They went on. He had less difficulty keeping awake now; the air was thinner, and the afternoon breeze was cool. In the hour before twilight they reached the head of the falls.

Shangri-la Station, seemingly unchanged, lay before him; three rectangular unequal blocks of dark shimmering plastic, a somber ziggurat rising on the western bank of the narrow gorge through which the river sped. The formal gardens of tropical plants, established by a forgotten sector chief at least forty years before, looked as though they were being carefully maintained. At each of the building's setbacks there was an outdoor veranda overlooking the river, and these, too, were bedecked with plants. Gundersen felt a dryness in his throat and a tightness in his loins. He said to Srin'gahar, "How long may we stay here?"

"How long do you wish to stay?"

"One day, two—I don't know yet. It depends on the welcome I get."

"We are not yet in a great hurry," said the nildor. "My friends and I will make camp in the bush. When it is time for you to go on, come to us."

The nildoror moved slowly into the shadows. Gundersen approached the station. At the entrance to the garden he paused. The trees here were gnarled and bowed, with long feathery gray fronds dangling down; highland flora was different from that to the south, although perpetual summer ruled here even as in the true tropics behind him. Lights glimmered within the station. Everything out here seemed surprisingly orderly; the contrast with the shambles of the serpent station and the nightmare decay of the fungoid station was sharp. Not even the hotel garden was this well tended. Four neat rows of fleshy, obscene-looking pink forest candles bordered the walkway that ran toward the building. Slender, stately globeflower trees, heavy with gigantic fruit, formed little groves to left and right. There were hullygully trees and bitterfruits—exotics here, imported from the steaming equatorial tropics—and the mighty swordflower trees in full bloom, lifting their long shiny stamens to the sky. Elegant glitterivy and spiceburr vines writhed along the ground, but not in any random way. Gundersen took a few steps farther in, and heard the soft sad sigh of a sensifrons bush, whose gentle hairy leaves coiled and shrank as he went by, opening warily when he had gone past, shutting again when he whirled to steal a quick glance. Two more steps, and he came to a low tree whose name he could not recall, with glossy red winged leaves that took flight, breaking free of their delicate stems and soaring away; instantly their replacements began to sprout. The garden was magical. Yet there were surprises here. Beyond the glitterivy he discovered a crescent patch of tiger-moss, the carnivorous ground cover native to the unfriendly central plateau. The moss had been transplanted to other parts of the planet—there was a patch of it growing out of control at the seacoast hotel—but Gundersen remembered that Seena abhorred it, as she abhorred all the productions of that forbidding plateau. Worse yet, looking upward so that he could follow the path of the gracefully gliding leaves, Gundersen saw great masses of quivering jelly, streaked with blue and red neural fibers, hanging from several of the biggest trees: more carnivores, also natives of the central plateau. What were those sinister things doing in this enchanted garden? A moment later he had a third proof that Seena's terror of the plateau had faded: across his path there ran one of the plump, thieving otter-like animals that had bedeviled them the time they had been marooned there. It halted a moment, nose twitching, cunning paws upraised, looking for something to seize. Gundersen hissed at it and it scuttled into the shrubbery.

Now a massive two-legged figure emerged from a shadowed corner and blocked his way. Gundersen thought at first it was a sulidor, but he realized it was merely a robot, probably a gardener. It said resonantly, "Man, why are you here?"

"As a visitor. I'm a traveler seeking lodging for the night."

"Does the woman expect you?"

"I'm sure she doesn't. But she'll be willing to see me. Tell her Edmund Gundersen is here."

The robot scanned him carefully. "I will tell her. Remain where you are and touch nothing."

Gundersen waited. What seemed like an unhealthily long span of time went by. The twilight deepened, and one moon appeared. Some of the trees in the garden became luminous. A serpent, of the sort once used as a source of venom, slid silently across the path just in front of Gundersen and vanished. The wind shifted, stirring the trees and bringing him the faint sounds of a conversation of nildoror somewhere not far inland from the riverbank.

Then the robot returned and said, "The woman will see you. Follow the path and enter the station."

Gundersen went up the steps. On the porch he noticed unfamiliar-looking potted plants, scattered casually as though awaiting transplantation to the garden. Several of them waved tendrils at him or wistfully flashed lights intended to bring curious prey fatally close. He went in, and, seeing no one on the ground floor, caught hold of a dangling laddercoil and let himself be spun up to the first veranda. He observed that the station was as flawlessly maintained within as without, every surface clean and bright, the decorative murals unfaded, the artifacts from many worlds still mounted properly in their niches. This station had always been a showplace, but he was surprised to see it so attractive in these years of the decay of Earth's presence on Belzagor.

"Seena?" he called.

He found her alone on the veranda, leaning over the rail. By the light of two moons he saw the deep cleft of her buttocks and thought she had chosen to greet him in the nude; but as she turned toward him he realized that a strange garment covered the front of her body. It was a pale, gelatinous sprawl, shapeless, purple-tinged, with the texture and sheen that he imagined an immense amoeba might have. The central mass of it embraced her belly and loins, leaving her hips and haunches bare; her left breast also was bare, but one broad pseudopod extended upward over the right one. The stuff was translucent, and Gundersen plainly could see the red eye of her covered nipple, and the narrow socket of her navel. It was also alive, to some degree, for it began to flow, apparently of its own will, sending out slow new strands that encircled her left thigh and right hip.

The eeriness of this clinging garment left him taken aback. Except for it, she appeared to be the Seena of old; she had gained some weight, and her breasts were heavier, her hips broader, yet she was still a handsome woman in the last bloom of youth. But the Seena of old would never have allowed such a bizarreness to touch her skin.

She regarded him steadily. Her lustrous black hair tumbled to her shoulders, as in the past. Her face was unlined. She faced him squarely and without shame, her feet firmly planted, her arms at ease, her head held high. "I thought you were never coming back here, Edmund," she said. Her voice had deepened, indicating some inner deepening as well. When he had last known her she had tended to speak too quickly, nervously pitching her tone too high, but now, calm and perfectly poised, she spoke with the resonance of a fine cello. "Why are you back?" she asked.

"It's a long story, Seena. I can't even understand all of it myself. May I stay here tonight?"

"Of course. How needless to ask!"

"You look so good, Seena. Somehow I expected—after eight years—"

"A hag?"

"Well, not exactly." His eyes met hers, and he was shaken abruptly by the rigidity he found there, a fixed and inflexible gaze, a beadiness that reminded him terrifyingly of the expression in the eyes of Dykstra and his woman at the last jungle station. "I—I don't know what I expected," he said.

"Time's been good to you also, Edmund. You have that stern, disciplined look, now—all the weakness burned away by years, only the core of manhood left. You've never looked better."

"Thank you."

"Won't you kiss me?" she asked.

"I understand you're a married woman."

She winced and tightened one fist. The thing she was wearing reacted also, deepening in color and shooting a pseudopod up to encircle, though not to conceal, her bare breast. "Where did you hear that?" she asked.

"At the coast. Van Beneker told me you married Jeff Kurtz."

"Yes. Not long after you left, as a matter of fact."

"I see. Is he here?"

She ignored his question. "Don't you *want* to kiss me? Or do you have a policy about kissing other men's wives?"

He forced a laugh. Awkwardly, self-consciously, he reached for her, taking her lightly by the shoulders and drawing her toward him. She was a tall woman. He inclined his head, trying to put his lips to hers without having any part of his body come in contact with the amoeba. She pulled back before the kiss.

"What are you afraid of?" she asked.

"What you're wearing makes me nervous."

"The slider?"

"If that's what it's called."

"It's what the sulidoror call it," Seena said. "It comes from the central plateau. It clings to one of the big mammals there and lives by metabolizing perspiration. Isn't it splendid?"

"I thought you hated the plateau."

"Oh, that was a long time ago. I've been there many times. I brought the slider back on the last trip. It's as much of a pet as it is something to wear. Look." She touched it lightly and it went through a series of color changes, expanding as it approached the blue end of the spectrum, contracting toward the red. At its greatest extension it formed a complete tunic covering Seena from throat to thighs. Gundersen became aware of something dark and pulsing at the heart of it, resting just above her loins, hiding the pubic triangle: its nerve-center, perhaps. "Why do you dislike it?" she asked. "Here. Put your hand on it." He made no move. She took his hand in hers and touched it to her side; he felt the slider's cool dry surface and was surprised that it was not slimy. Easily Seena moved his hand upward until it came to the heavy globe of a breast, and instantly the slider contracted, leaving the firm warm flesh bare to his fingers. He cupped it in a moment, and, uneasy, withdrew his hand. Her nipples had hardened; her nostrils had flared.

He said, "The slider's very interesting. But I don't like it on you."

"Very well." She touched herself at the base of her belly, just above the organism's core. It shrank inward and flowed down her leg in one swift rippling movement gliding away and collecting itself at the far side of the veranda. "Is that better?" Seena asked, naked, now, sweat-shiny, moist-lipped.

The coarseness of her approach startled him. Neither he nor she had ever worried much about nudity, but there was a deliberate sexual aggressiveness about this kind of self-display that seemed out of keeping with what he regarded as her character. They were old friends, yes; they had once been lovers for several years; they had been married in all but the name for many months of that time; but even so the ambiguity of their parting should have destroyed whatever intimacy once existed. And, leaving the question of her marriage to Kurtz out of it, the fact that they had not seen one another for eight years seemed to him to dictate the necessity of a more gradual return to physical closeness. He felt that by making herself pantingly available to him within minutes of his unexpected arrival she was committing a breach not of morals but of esthetics.

"Put something on," he said quietly. "And not the slider. I can't have a serious conversation with you while you're waving all those jiggling temptations in my face."

"Poor conventional Edmund. All right. Have you had

dinner?''

''No.''

''I'll have it served out here. And drinks. I'll be right back.''

She entered the building. The slider remained behind on the veranda; it rolled tentatively toward Gundersen, as though offering to climb up and be worn by him for a while, but he glared at it and enough feeling got through to make the plateau creature move hurriedly away. A minute later a robot emerged, bearing a tray on which two golden cocktails sat. It offered one drink to Gundersen, set the other on the railing, and noiselessly departed. Then Seena returned, chastely clad in a soft gray shift that descended from her shoulders to her shins.

''Better?'' she asked.

''For now.'' They touched glasses; she smiled; they put their drinks to their lips. ''You remembered that I don't like sonic snouts,'' he said.

''I forget very little, Edmund.''

''What's it like, living up here?''

''Serene. I never imagined that my life could be so calm. I read a good deal; I help the robots tend the garden; occasionally there are guests; sometimes I travel. Weeks often go by without my seeing another human being.''

''What about your husband?''

''Weeks often go by without my seeing another human being,'' she said.

''You're alone here? You and the robots?''

''Quite alone.''

''But the other Company people must come here fairly frequently.''

''Some do. There aren't many of us left now,'' Seena said. ''Less than a hundred, I imagine. About six at the Sea of Dust. Van Beneker down by the hotel. Four or five at the old rift station. And so on—little islands of Earthmen widely scattered. There's a sort of a social circuit, but it's a sparse one.''

''Is this what you wanted when you chose to stay here?'' Gundersen asked.

''I didn't know what I wanted, except that I wanted to stay.

But I'd do it again. Knowing everything I know, I'd do it just the same way."

He said, "At the station just south of here, below the falls, I saw Harold Dykstra—"

"Henry Dykstra."

"Henry. And a woman I didn't know."

"Pauleen Mazor. She was one of the customs girls, in the time of the Company. Henry and Pauleen are my closest neighbors, I guess. But I haven't seen them in years. I never go south of the falls any more, and they haven't come here."

"They're dead, Seena."

"Oh?"

"It was like stepping into a nightmare. A sulidor led me to them. The station was a wreck, mold and fungoids everywhere, and something was hatching inside them, the larvae of some kind of basket-shaped red sponge that hung on a wall and dripped black oil—"

"Things like that happen," Seena said, not sounding disturbed. "Sooner or later this planet catches everyone, though always in a different way."

"Dykstra was unconscious, and the woman was begging to be put out of her misery, and—"

"You said they were dead."

"Not when I got there. I told the sulidor to kill them. There was no hope of saving them. He split them open, and then I used my torch on them."

"We had to do that for Gio' Salamone, too," Seena said. "He was staying at Fire Point, and went out into the Sea of Dust and got some kind of crystalline parasite into a cut. When Kurtz and Ced Cullen found him, he was all cubes and prisms, outcroppings of the most beautiful iridescent minerals breaking through his skin everywhere. And he was still alive. For a while. Another drink?"

"Please. Yes."

She summoned the robot. It was quite dark, now. A third moon had appeared.

In a low voice Seena said, "I'm so happy you came tonight, Edmund. It was such a wonderful surprise."

"Kurtz isn't here now?"

"No," she said. "He's away, and I don't know when he'll

be back."

"How has it been for him, living here?"

"I think he's been quite happy, generally speaking. Of course, he's a very strange man."

"He is," Gundersen said.

"He's got a quality of sainthood about him, I think."

"He would have been a dark and chilling saint, Seena."

"Some saints are. They don't all have to be St. Francis of Assisi."

"Is cruelty one of the desirable traits of a saint?"

"Kurtz saw cruelty as a dynamic force. He made himself an artist of cruelty."

"So did the Marquis de Sade. Nobody's canonized *him.*"

"You know what I mean," she said. "You once spoke of Kurtz to me, and you called him a fallen angel. That's exactly right. I saw him out among the nildoror, dancing with hundreds of them, and they came to him and practically worshipped him. There he was, talking to them, caressing them. And yet also doing the most destructive things to them as well, but they loved it."

"What kind of destructive things?"

"They don't matter. I doubt that you'd approve. He—gave them drugs, sometimes."

"The serpent venom?"

"Sometimes."

"Where is he now? Out playing with the nildoror?"

"He's been ill for a while." The robot now was serving dinner. Gundersen frowned at the strange vegetables on his plate. "They're perfectly safe," Seena said "I grow them myself, in back. I'm quite the farmer."

"I don't remember any of these."

"They're from the plateau."

Gundersen shook his head. "When I think of how disgusted you were by the plateau, how strange and frightening it seemed to you that time we had to crash-land there—"

"I was a child then. When was it, eleven years ago? Soon after I met you. I was only twenty years old. But on Belzagor you must defeat what frightens you, or you will be defeated. I went back to the plateau. Again and again. It ceased to be strange to me, and so it ceased to frighten me, and so I came to love it. And brought many of its plants and animals back here to live with me. It's so very different from the rest of Belzagor—cut off from everything else, almost alien."

"You went there with Kurtz?"

"Sometimes. And sometimes with Ced Cullen. And most often alone."

"Cullen," Gundersen said. "Do you see him often?"

"Oh, yes. He and Kurtz and I have been a kind of triumvirate. My other husband, almost. I mean, in a spiritual way. Physical too, at times, but that's not as important"

"Where is Cullen now?" he asked, looking intently into her harsh and glossy eyes.

Her expression darkened. "In the north. The mist country."

"What's he doing there?"

"Why don't you go ask him?" she suggested.

"I'd like to do just that," Gundersen said. "I'm on my way up mist country, actually, and this is just a sentimental stop on the way. I'm traveling with five nildoror going for rebirth. They're camped in the bush out there somewhere."

She opened a flask of a musky gray-green wine and gave him some. "Why do you want to go to the mist country?" she asked tautly.

"Curiosity. The same motive that sent Cullen up there, I guess."

"I don't think his motive was curiosity."

"Will you amplify that?"

"I'd rather not," she said.

The conversation sputtered into silence. Talking to her led only in circles, he thought. This new serenity of hers could be maddening. She told him only what she cared to tell him, playing with him, seemingly relishing the touch of her sweet contralto voice on the night air, communicating no information at all. This was not a Seena he had ever known. The girl he had loved had been resilient and strong, but not crafty or secretive; there had been an innocence about her that seemed totally lost now. Kurtz might not be the only fallen angel on this planet.

He said suddenly, "The fourth moon has risen!"

"Yes. Of course. Is that so amazing?"

"One rarely sees four, even in this latitude."

"It happens at least ten times a year. Why waste your awe? In a little while the fifth one will be up, and—"

Gundersen gasped. "Is that what tonight is?"

"The Night of Five Moons, yes."

"No one told me!"

"Perhaps you never asked."

"Twice I missed it because I was at Fire Point. One year I was at sea, and once I was in the southern mist country, the time that the copter went down. And so on and on. I managed to see it only once, Seena, right here, ten years ago, with you. When things were at their best for us. And now, to come in by accident and have it happen!"

"I thought you had arranged to be here deliberately. To commemorate that other time."

"No. No. Pure coincidence."

"Happy coincidence, then."

"When does it rise?"

"Perhaps an hour."

He watched the four bright dots swimming through the sky. It was so long ago that he had forgotten where the fifth moon should be coming from. Its orbit was retrograde, he thought. It was the most brilliant of the moons, too, with a high-albedo surface of ice, smooth as a mirror.

Seena filled his glass again. They had finished eating. "Excuse me," she said. "I'll be back soon."

Alone, he studied the sky and tried to comprehend this strangely altered Seena, this mysterious woman whose body had grown more voluptuous and whose soul, it seemed, had turned to stone. He saw now that the stone had been in her all along: at their breakup, for example, when he had put in for her transfer to Earth, and she had absolutely refused to leave Holman's World. I love you, she had said, and I'll always love you, but this is where I stay. Why? Why? Because I want to stay, she told him. And she stayed; and he was just as stubborn, and left without her; and they slept together on the beach beneath the hotel on his last night, so that the warmth of her body was still on his skin when he boarded the ship that took him away. She loved him and he loved her, but they broke apart, for he saw no future on this world, and she saw all her future on it. And she had married Kurtz. And she had explored the unknown plateau. And she spoke in a rich deep new voice, and let alien amoebas clasp her loins, and shrugged at the news that two nearby Earthmen had died a horrible death. Was she still Seena, or some subtle counterfeit?

Nildoror sounds drifted out of the darkness. Gundersen heard another sound, too, closer by, a kind of stifled snorting grunt that was wholly unfamiliar to him. It seemed like a cry of pain, though perhaps that was his imagination. Probably it was one of Seena's plateau beasts, snuffling around searching for tasty roots in the garden. He heard it twice more, and then not again.

Time went by and Seena did not return.

Then he saw the fifth moon float placidly into the sky, the size of a large silver coin, and so bright that it dazzled the eye. About it the other four danced, two of them mere tiny dots, two of them more imposing, and the shadows of the moonslight shattered and shattered again as planes of brilliance intersected. The heavens poured light upon the land in icy cascades. He gripped the rail of the veranda and silently begged the moons to hold their pattern; like Faust he longed to cry out to the fleeting moment, stay, stay forever, stay, you are beautiful! But the moons shifted, driven by the unseen Newtonian machinery; he knew that in another hour two of them would be gone and the magic would ebb. Where was Seena?

"Edmund?" she said, from behind him.

She was bare, again, and once more the slider was on her body, covering her loins, sending a long thin projection up to encompass only the nipple of each ripe breast. The light of the five moons made her tawny skin glitter and shine. Now she did not seem coarse to him, nor overly aggressive; she was perfect in her nudity, and the moment was perfect, and unhesitatingly he went to her. Quickly he dropped his clothing. He put his hands to her hips, touching the slider, and the strange creature understood, flowing obediently from her body, a chastity belt faithless to its task. She leaned toward him, her breasts swaying like fleshy bells, and he kissed her, here, here, here, there, and they sank to the veranda floor, to the cold smooth stone.

Her eyes remained open, and colder than the floor, colder than the shifting light of the moons, even at the moment when he entered her.

But there was nothing cold about her embrace. Their bodies thrashed and tangled, and her skin was soft and her kiss was hungry, and the years rolled away until it was the old time again, the happy time. At the highest moment he was dimly aware of that strange grunting sound once more. He clasped her fiercely and let his eyes close.

Afterward they lay side by side, wordless in the moons-light, until the brilliant fifth moon had completed its voyage across the sky and the Night of the Five Moons had become as any other night.

Ten

HE SLEPT BY himself in one of the guest rooms on the topmost level of the station. Awakening unexpectedly early, he watched the sunrise coming over the gorge, and went down to walk through the gardens, which still were glistening with dew. He strolled as far as the edge of the river, looking for his nildoror companions; but they were not to be seen. For a long time he stood beside the river watching the irresistible downward sweep of that immense volume of water. Were there fish in the river here, he wondered? How did they avoid being carried over the brink? Surely anything once caught up in that mighty flow would have no choice but to follow the route dictated for it, and be swept toward the terrible drop.

He went back finally to the station. By the light of morning Seena's garden seemed less sinister to him. Even the plants and animals of the plateau appeared merely strange, not menacing; each geographical district of this world had its own typical fauna and flora, that was all, and it was not the fault of the plateau's creatures that man had not chosen to make himself at ease among them. A robot met him on the first veranda and offered him breakfast.

"I'll wait for the woman," Gundersen said.

"She will not appear until much later in the morning."

"That's odd. She never used to sleep that much."

"She is with the man," the robot volunteered. "She stays with him and comforts him at this hour."

"What man?"

"The man Kurtz, her husband."

Gundersen said, amazed, "Kurtz is here at the station?"

"He lies ill in his room."

She said he was away somewhere, Gundersen thought. She didn't know when he'd be coming back.

Gundersen said, "Was he in his room last night?"

"He was."

"How long has he been back from his last journey away from here?"

"One year at the solstice," the robot said. "Perhaps you should consult the woman on these matters. She will be with you after a while. Shall I bring breakfast?"

"Yes," Gundersen said.

But Seena was not long in arriving. Ten minutes after he had finished the juices, fruits, and fried fish that the robot had brought him, she appeared on the veranda, wearing a filmy white wrap through which the contours of her body were evident. She seemed to have slept well. Her skin was clear and glowing, her stride was vigorous, her dark hair streamed buoyantly in the morning breeze; but yet the curiously rigid and haunted expression of her eyes was unchanged, and clashed with the innocence of the new day.

He said, "The robot told me not to wait breakfast for you. It said you wouldn't be down for a long while."

"That's all right. I'm not usually down this early, it's true. Come for a swim?"

"In the river?"

"No, silly!" She stripped away her wrap and ran down the steps into the garden. He sat frozen a moment, caught up in the rhythms of her swinging arms, her jouncing buttocks; then he followed her. At a twist in the path that he had not noticed before, she turned to the left and halted at a circular pool that appeared to have been punched out of the living rock on the river's flank. As he reached it, she launched herself in a fine arching dive, and appeared to hang suspended a moment, floating above the dark water, her breasts drawn into a startling roundness by gravity's pull. Then she went under. Before she came up for breath, Gundersen was naked and in the pool beside her. Even in this mild climate the water was bitterly cold.

"It comes from an underground spring," she told him. "Isn't it wonderful? Like a rite of purification."

A gray tendril rose from the water behind her, tipped with rubbery claws. Gundersen could find no words to warn her. He pointed with short stabbing motions of two fingers and made hollow chittering noises of horror. A second tendril spiraled out of the depths and hovered over her. Smiling, Seena turned, and seemed to fondle some large creature; there was a thrashing in the water and then the tendrils slipped out of view.

"What was *that?*"

"The monster of the pool," she said. "Ced Cullen brought it for me as a birthday present two years ago. It's a plateau medusa. They live in lakes and sting things."

"How big is it?"

"Oh, the size of a big octopus, I'd say. Very affectionate. I wanted Ced to catch me a mate for it, but he didn't get around to it before he went north, and I suppose I'll have to do it myself before long. The monster's lonely." She pulled herself out of the pool and sprawled out on a slab of smooth black rock to dry in the sun. Gundersen followed her. From this side of the pool, with the light penetrating the water at just the right angle, he was able to see a massive many-limbed shape far below. Seena's birthday present.

He said, "Can you tell me where I can find Ced now?"

"In the mist country."

"I know. That's a big place. Any particular part?"

She rolled over onto her back and flexed her knees. Sunlight made prisms of the droplets of water on her breasts. After a long silence she said, "Why do you want to find him so badly?"

"I'm making a sentimental journey to see old friends. Ced and I were very close, once. Isn't that reason enough for me to go looking for him?"

"It's no reason to betray him, is it?"

He stared at her. The fierce eyes now were closed; the heavy mounds of her breasts rose and fell slowly, serenely. "What do you mean by that?" he asked.

"Didn't the nildoror put you up to going after him?"

"What kind of crazy talk is that?" he blurted, not sounding convincingly indignant even to himself.

"Why must you pretend?" she said, still speaking from within that impregnable core of total assurance. "The nildoror want him brought back from there. By treaty they're prevented from going up there and getting him themselves. The sulidoror don't feel like extraditing him. Certainly none of the Earthmen living on this planet will fetch him. Now, as an outsider you need nildoror permission to enter the mist country, and since you're a stickler for the rules you probably applied for such permission, and there's no special reason why the nildoror should grant favors to you unless you agree to do something for them in return. Eh? Q.E.D."

"Who told you all this?"

"Believe me, I worked it all out for myself."

He propped his head on his hand and reached out admiringly with the other hand to touch her thigh. Her skin was dry and warm now. He let his hand rest lightly, and then not so lightly, on the firm flesh. Seena showed no reaction. Softly he said, "Is it too late for us to make a treaty?"

"What kind?"

"A nonaggression pact. We've been fencing since I got here. Let's end the hostilities. I've been hiding things from you, and you've been hiding things from me, and what good is it? Why can't we simply help one another? We're two human beings on a world that's much stranger and more dangerous than most people suspect, and if we can't supply a little mutual aid and comfort, what are the ties of humanity worth?"

She said quietly,

> "Ah, love, let us be true
> To one another: for the world, which seems
> To lie before us like a land of dreams,
> So various, so beautiful, so new—"

The words of the old poem flowed up from the well of his memory. His voice cut in:

> "—Hath really neither joy, nor love, nor light,
> Nor certitude, nor peace, nor help for pain;
> And we are here as on a darkling plain
> Swept with confused alarms of struggle and flight
> Where—where—"

"'Where ignorant armies clash by night,'" she finished for him. "Yes. How like you it is, Edmund, to fumble your lines just at the crucial moment, just at the final climax."

"Then there's to be no nonaggression pact?"

"I'm sorry. I shouldn't have said that." She turned toward him, took his hand from her thigh, pressed it tenderly between her breasts, brushed her lips against it. "All right, we've been playing little games. They're over, and now we'll speak only truth, but you go first. Did the nildoror ask you to bring Ced Cullen out of the mist country?"

"Yes," Gundersen said. "It was the condition of my entry."

"And you promised you'd do it?"

"I made certain reservations and qualifications, Seena. If he won't go willingly, I'm not bound by honor to force him. But I do have to find him, at least. That much I've pledged. So I ask you again to tell me where I should look."

"I don't know," she said. "I have no idea. He could be anywhere at all up there."

"Is this the truth?"

"The truth," she said, and for a moment the harshness was gone from her eyes, and her voice was the voice of a woman and not that of a cello.

"Can you tell me, at least, why he fled, why they want him so eagerly?"

She was slow in replying. Finally she said, "About a year ago, he went down into the central plateau on one of his regular collecting trips. He was planning to get me another medusa, he said. Most of the time I went with him into the plateau, but this time Kurtz was ill and I had to stay behind. Ced went to a part of the plateau we had never visited before, and there he found a group of nildoror taking part in some kind of religious ceremony. He stumbled right into them and evidently he profaned the ritual."

"Rebirth?" Gundersen asked.

"No, they do rebirth only in the mist country. This was something else, something almost as serious, it seems. The nildoror were furious. Ced barely escaped alive. He came back here and said he was in great trouble, that the nildoror wanted him, that he had committed some sort of sacrilege and had to take sanctuary. Then he went north, with a posse of nildoror chasing him right to the border. I haven't heard anything since. I have no contact with the mist country. And that's all I can tell you."

"You haven't told me what sort of sacrilege he committed," Gundersen pointed out.

"I don't know it. I don't know what kind of ritual it was, or what he did to interrupt it. I've told you only as much as he told me. Will you believe that?"

"I'll believe it," he said. He smiled. "Now let's play another game, and this time I'll take the lead. Last night you told me that Kurtz was off on a trip, that you hadn't seen him for a long time and didn't know when he'd be back. You also said he'd been sick, but you brushed over that pretty quickly. This morning, the robot who brought me breakfast said that you'd be late coming down, because Kurtz was ill and you were with him in his room, as you were every morning at this time. Robots don't ordinarily lie."

"The robot wasn't lying. I was."

"Why?"

"To shield him from you," Seena said. "He's in very bad shape, and I don't want him to be disturbed. And I knew that if I told you he was here, you'd want to see him. He isn't strong enough for visitors. It was an innocent lie, Edmund."

"What's wrong with him?"

"We aren't sure. You know, there isn't much of a medical service left on this planet. I've got a diagnostat, but it gave me no useful data when I put him through it. I suppose I could describe his disease as a kind of cancer. Only cancer isn't what he has."

"Can you describe the symptoms?"

"What's the use? His body began to change. He became something strange and ugly and frightening, and you don't need to know the details. If you thought that what had happened to Dykstra and Pauleen was horrible, you'd be rocked to your roots by Kurtz. But I won't let you see him. It's as much to shield you from him as the other way around. You'll be better off not seeing him." Seena sat up, cross-legged on the rock, and began to untangle the wet snarled strands of her hair. Gundersen thought he had never seen her looking as beautiful as she looked right at this moment, clothed only in alien sunlight, her flesh taut and ripe and glowing, her body supple, full-blown, mature. And the fierceness of her eyes, the one jarring discordancy? Had that come from viewing, each morning, the horror that Kurtz now was? She said after a long while, "Kurtz is being punished for his sins."

"Do you really believe that?"

"I do," she said. "I believe that there are such things as sins, and that there is retribution for sin."

"And that an old man with a white beard is up there in the sky, keeping score on everyone, running the show, tallying up an adultery here, a lie there, a spot of gluttony, a little pride?"

"I have no idea who runs the show," said Seena. "I'm not even sure that anyone does. Don't mislead yourself, Edmund: I'm not trying to import medieval theology to Belzagor. I won't give you the Father, the Son, and the Holy Ghost, and say that all over the universe certain fundamental principles hold true. I simply say that here on Belzagor we live in the presence of certain moral absolutes, native to this planet, and if a stranger comes to Belzagor and transgresses against those absolutes, he'll regret it. This world is not ours, never was, never will be, and we who live here are in a constant state of peril, because we don't understand the basic rules."

"What sins did Kurtz commit?"

"It would take me all morning to name them," she said. "Some were sins against the nildoror, and some were sins against his own spirit."

"We all committed sins against the nildoror," Gundersen said.

"In a sense, yes. We were proud and foolish, and we failed to see them for what they were, and we used them unkindly. That's a sin, yes, of course, a sin that our ancestors committed all over Earth long before we went into space. But Kurtz had a greater capacity for sin than the rest of us, because he was a greater man. Angels have farther to fall, once they fall."

"What did Kurtz do to the nildoror? Kill them? Dissect them? Whip them?"

"Those are sins against their bodies," said Seena. "He did worse."

"Tell me."

"Do you know what used to go on at the serpent station, south of the spaceport?"

"I was there for a few weeks with Kurtz and Salamone," Gundersen said. "Long ago, when I was very new here, when you were still a child on Earth. I watched the two of them call serpents out of the jungle, and milk the raw venom from them, and give the venom to nildoror to drink. And drink the venom themselves."

"And what happened then?"

He shoo: his head. "I've never been able to understand it. When I tried it with them, I had the illusion that the three of us were turning into nildoror. And that three nildoror had turned into us. I had a trunk, four legs, tusks, spines. Everything looked different; I was seeing through nildoror eyes. Then it ended, and I was in my own body again, and I felt a terrible rush of guilt, of shame. I had no way of knowing whether it had been a real bodily metamorphosis or just hallucination."

"It was hallucination," Seena told him. "The venom opened your mind, your soul, and enabled you to enter the nildor consciousness, at the same time that the nildor was entering yours. For a little while that nildor thought he was Edmund Gundersen. Such a dream is great ecstasy to a nildor."

"Is this Kurtz's sin, then? To give ecstasy to nildoror?"

"The serpent venom," Seena said, "is also used in the rebirth ceremony. What you and Kurtz and Salamone were doing down there in the jungle was going through a very mild—*very* mild—version of rebirth. And so were the nildoror. But it was blasphemous rebirth for them, for many reasons. First, because it was held in the wrong place. Second, because it was done without the proper rituals. Third, because the celebrants who guided the nildoror were men, not sulidoror, and so the entire thing became a wicked parody of the most sacred act this planet has. By giving those nildoror the venom, Kurtz was tempting them to dabble in something diabolical, literally diabolical. Few nildoror can resist that temptation. He found pleasure in the act—both in the hallucinations that the venom gave him, and in the tempting of the nildoror. I think that he enjoyed the tempting even more than the hallucinations, and that was his worst sin, for through it he led innocent nildoror into what passes for damnation on this planet. In twenty years on Belzagor he inveigled hundreds, perhaps thousands, of nildoror into sharing a bowl of venom with him. Finally his presence became intolerable, and his own hunger for evil became the source of his destruction. And now he lies upstairs, neither living nor dead, no longer a danger to anything on Belzagor."

"You think that staging the local equivalent of a Black Mass is what brought Kurtz to whatever destiny it is that you're hiding from me?"

"I know it," Seena replied. She got to her feet, stretched voluptuously, and beckoned to him. "Let's go back to the station now."

As though this were time's first dawn they walked naked through the garden, close together, the warmth of the sun and the warmth of her body stirring him and raising a fever in him. Twice he considered pulling her to the ground and taking her amidst these alien shrubs, and twice he held back, not knowing why. When they were a dozen meters from the house he felt desire climb again, and he turned to her and put his hand on her breast. But she said, "Tell me one more thing, first."

"If I can."

"Why have you come back to Belzagor? Really. What draws you to the mist country?"

He said, "If you believe in sin, you must believe in the possibility of redemption from sin."

"Yes."

"Well, then, I have a sin on my conscience, too. Perhaps not as grave a sin as the sins of Kurtz, but enough to trouble me, and I've come back here as an act of expiation."

"How have you sinned?" she asked.

"I sinned against the nildoror in the ordinary Earthman way, by collaborating in their enslavement, by patronizing them, by failing to credit their intelligence and their complexity. In particular I sinned by preventing seven nildoror from reaching rebirth on time. Do you remember, when the Monroe dam broke, and I commandeered those pilgrims for a labor detail? I used a fusion torch to make them obey, and on my account they missed rebirth. I didn't know that if they were late for rebirth they'd lose their turn, and if I had known I wouldn't have thought it mattered. Sin within sin within sin. I left here feeling stained. Those seven nildoror bothered me in my dreams. I realized that I had to come back and try to cleanse my soul."

"What kind of expiation do you have in mind?" she asked.

His eyes had difficulty meeting hers. He lowered them, but that was worse, for the nakedness of her unnerved him even more, as they stood together in the sunlight outside the station. He forced his glance upward again.

He said, "I've determined to find out what rebirth is, and to take part in it. I'm going to offer myself to the sulidoror as a candidate."

"No."

"Seena, what's wrong? You—"

She trembled. Her cheeks were blazing, and the rush of scarlet spread even to her breasts. She bit her lip, spun away from him, and turned back. "It's insanity," she said. "Rebirth isn't something for Earthmen. Why do you think you can possibly expiate anything by getting yourself mixed up in an alien religion, by surrendering yourself to a process none of us knows anything about, by—"

"I have to, Seena."

"Don't be crazy."

"It's an obsession. You're the first person I've ever spoken to about it. The nildoror I'm traveling with aren't aware of it. I can't stop. I owe this planet a life, and I'm here to pay. I have to go, regardless of the consequences."

She said, "Come inside the station with me." Her voice was flat, mechanical, empty.

"Why?"

"Come inside."

He followed her silently in. She led him to the middle level of the building, and into a corridor blocked by one of her robot guardians. At a nod from her the robot stepped aside. Outside a room at the rear she paused and put her hand to the door's scanner. The door rolled back. Seena gestured to him to walk in with her.

He heard the grunting, snorting sound that he had heard the night before, and now there was no doubt in his mind that it had been a cry of terrible throttled pain.

"This is the room where Kurtz spends his time," Seena said. She drew a curtain that had divided the room. "And this is Kurtz," she said.

"It isn't possible," Gundersen murmured. "How—how—"

"How did he get that way?"

"Yes."

"As he grew older he began to feel remorse for the crimes he had committed. He suffered greatly in his guilt, and last year he resolved to undertake an act of expiation. He decided to travel to the mist country and undergo rebirth. This is what they brought back to me. This is what a human being looks like, Edmund, when he's undergone rebirth."

Eleven

WHAT GUNDERSEN BEHELD was apparently human, and probably it had once even been Jeff Kurtz. The absurd length of the body was surely Kurtzlike, for the figure in the bed seemed to be a man and a half long, as if an extra section of vertebrae and perhaps a second pair of femurs had been spliced in. The skull was plainly Kurtz's too: mighty white dome, jutting brow-ridges. The ridges were even more prominent than Gundersen remembered. They rose above Kurtz's closed eyes like barricades guarding against some invasion from the north. But the thick black brows that had covered those ridges were gone. So were the lush, almost feminine eyelashes.

Below the forehead the face was unrecognizable.

It was as if everything had been heated in a crucible and allowed to melt and run. Kurtz's fine high-bridged nose was now a rubbery smear, so snoutlike that Gundersen was jolted by its resemblance to a sulidor's. His wide mouth now had slack, pendulous lips that drooped open, revealing toothless gums. His chin sloped backward in pithecanthropoid style. Kurtz's cheekbones were flat and broad, wholly altering the planes of his face.

Seena drew the coverlet down to display the rest. The body in the bed was utterly hairless, a long boiled-looking pink thing like a giant slug. All superfluous flesh was gone, and the skin lay like a shroud over plainly visible ribs and muscles. The proportions of the body were wrong. Kurtz's waist was an impossibly great distance from his chest, and his legs, though long, were not nearly as long as they should have been; his ankles seemed to crowd his knees. His toes had fused, so that his feet terminated in bestial pads. Perhaps by compensation, his fingers had added extra joints and were great spidery things that flexed and clenched in irregular rhythms. The attachment of his arms to his torso appeared strange, though it was not until Gundersen saw Kurtz slowly rotate his left arm through a 360-degree twist that he realized the armpit must have been reconstructed into some kind of versatile ball-and-socket arrangement.

Kurtz struggled desperately to speak, blurting words in a language Gundersen had never heard. His eyeballs visibly stirred beneath his lids. His tongue slipped forth to moisten his lips. Something like a three-lobed Adam's apple bobbed in his throat. Briefly he humped his body, drawing the skin tight over curiously broadened bones. He continued to speak. Occasionally an intelligible word in English or nildororu emerged, embedded in a flow of gibberish: "River . . . death . . . lost . . . horror . . . river . . . cave . . . warm . . . lost . . . warm . . . smash . . . black . . . go . . . god . . . horror . . . born . . . lost . . . born. . . ."

"What is he saying?" Gundersen asked.

"No one knows. Even when we can understand the words, he doesn't make sense. And mostly we can't even understand the words. He speaks the language of the world where he must live now. It's a very private language."

"Has he been conscious at all since he's been here?"

"Not really," Seena said. "Sometimes his eyes are open, but he never responds to anything around him. Come. Look." She went to the bed and drew Kurtz's eyelids open. Gundersen saw eyes that had no whites at all. From rim to rim their shining surfaces were a deep, lustrous black, dappled by random spots of light blue. He held three fingers up before those eyes and waved his hand from side to side. Kurtz took no notice. Seena released the lids, and the eyes remained open, even when the tips of Gundersen's fingers approached quite closely. But as

Gundersen withdrew his hand, Kurtz lifted his right hand and seized Gundersen's wrist. The grotesquely elongated fingers encircled the wrist completely, met, and coiled halfway around it again. Slowly and with tremendous strength Kurtz pulled Gundersen down until he was kneeling beside the bed.

Now Kurtz spoke only in English. As before he seemed to be in desperate anguish, forcing the words out of some nightmare recess, with no perceptible accenting or punctuation: "Water sleep death save sleep sleep fire love water dream cold sleep plan rise fall rise fall rise rise rise." After a moment he added, "Fall." Then the flow of nonsense syllables returned and the fingers relinquished their fierce grip on Gundersen's wrist.

Seena said, "He seemed to be telling us something. I never heard him speak so many consecutive intelligible words."

"But what was he saying?"

"I can't tell you that. But a meaning was there."

Gundersen nodded. The tormented Kurtz had delivered his testament, his blessing: *Sleep plan rise fall rise fall rise rise rise. Fall.* Perhaps it even made sense.

"And he reacted to your presence," Seena went on. "He saw you, he took your arm! Say something to him. See if you can get his attention again."

"Jeff?" Gundersen whispered, kneeling. "Jeff, do you remember me? Edmund Gundersen. I've come back, Jeff. Can you hear anything I'm saying? If you understand me, Jeff, raise your right hand again."

Kurtz did not raise his hand. He uttered a strangled moan, low and appalling; then his eyes slowly closed and he lapsed into a rigid silence. Muscles rippled beneath his altered skin. Beads of acrid sweat broke from his pores. Gundersen got to his feet shortly and walked away.

"How long was he ~~up~~ there?" he asked.

"Close to half a year. I thought he was dead. Then two sulidoror brought him back, on a kind of stretcher."

"Changed like this?"

"Changed. And here he lies. He's changed much more than you imagine," Seena said. "Inside, everything's new and different. He's got almost no digestive tract at all. Solid food is impossible for him; I give him fruit juices. His heart has extra chambers. His lungs are twice as big as they should be. The diagnostat couldn't tell me a thing, because he didn't correspond to any of the parameters for a human body."

"And this happened to him in rebirth?"

"In rebirth, yes. They take a drug, and it changes them. And it works on humans too. It's the same drug they use on Earth for organ regeneration, the venom, but here they use a stronger dose and the body runs wild. If you go up there, Edmund, this is what'll happen to you."

"How do you *know* it was rebirth that did this to him?"

"I know."

"How?"

"That's what he said he was going up there for. And the sulidoror who brought him back said he had undergone rebirth."

"Maybe they were lying. Maybe rebirth is one thing, a beneficial thing, and there's another thing, a harmful thing, which they gave to Kurtz because he had been so evil."

"You're deceiving yourself," Seena said. "There's only one process, and this is its result."

"Possibly different people respond differently to the process, then. If there is only one process. But I still say you can't be sure that it was rebirth that actually did this to him."

"Don't talk nonsense!"

"I mean it. Maybe something within Kurtz made him turn out like this, and I'd turn out another way. A better way."

"Do you *want* to be changed, Edmund?"

"I'd risk it."

"You'd cease to be human!"

"I've tried being human for quite a while. Maybe it's time to try something else."

"I won't let you go," Seena said.

"You won't? What claim do you have on me?"

"I've already lost Jeff to them. If you go up there

too—''

''Yes?''

She faltered. ''All right. I've got no way to threaten you. But don't go.''

''I have to.''

''You're just like him! Puffed up with the importance of your own supposed sins. Imagining the need for some kind of ghastly redemption. It's sick, don't you see? You just want to hurt yourself, in the worst possible way.'' Her eyes glittered even more brightly. ''Listen to me. If you need to suffer, I'll help you. You want me to whip you? Stamp on you? If you've got to play masochist, I'll play sadist for you. I'll give you all the torment you want. You can wallow in it. But don't go up mist country. That's carrying a game too far, Edmund.''

''You don't understand, Seena.''

''Do you?''

''Perhaps I will, when I come back from there.''

''You'll come back like *him!*'' she screamed. She rushed toward Kurtz's bed. ''Look at him! Look at those feet! Look at his eyes! His mouth, his nose, his fingers, his everything! He isn't human any more. Do you want to lie there like him—muttering nonsense, living in some weird dream all day and all night?''

Gundersen wavered. Kurtz *was* appalling; was the obsession so strong in him that he wanted to undergo the same transformation?

''I have to go,'' he said, less firmly than before.

''He's living in hell,'' Seena said. ''You'll be there too.''

She came to Gundersen and pressed herself against him. He felt the hot tips of her breasts grazing his skin; her hands clawed his back desperately; her thighs touched his. A great sadness came over him, for all that Seena once had meant to him, for all that she had been, for what she had become, for what her life must be like with this monster to care for. He was shaken by a vision of the lost and irrecoverable past, of the dark and uncertain present, of the bleak, frightening future. Again he wavered. Then he gently pushed her away from him. ''I'm sorry,'' he said. ''I'm going."

"Why? Why? What a *waste!*" Tears trickled down her cheeks. "If you need a religion," she said, "pick an Earth religion. There's no reason why you have to—"

"There is a reason," Gundersen said. He drew her close to him again and very lightly kissed her eyelids, and then her lips. Then he kissed her between the breasts and released her. He walked over to Kurtz and stood for a moment looking down, trying to come to terms with the man's bizarre metamorphosis. Now he noticed something he had not observed earlier: the thickened texture of the skin of Kurtz's back, as if dark little plaques were sprouting on both sides of his spine. No doubt there were many other changes as well, apparent only on a close inspection. Kurtz's eyes opened once again, and the black glossy orbs moved, as if seeking to meet Gundersen's eyes. He stared down at them, at the pattern of blue speckles against the shining solid background. Kurtz said, amidst many sounds Gundersen could not comprehend, "Dance . . . live . . . seek . . . die . . . die."

It was time to leave.

Walking past the motionless, rigid Seena, Gundersen went out of the room. He stepped onto the veranda and saw that his five nildoror were gathered outside the station, in the garden, with a robot uneasily watching lest they begin ripping up the rarities for fodder. Gundersen called out, and Srin'gahar looked up.

"I'm ready," Gundersen said. "We can leave as soon as I have my things."

He found his clothes and prepared to depart. Seena came to him again: she was dressed in a clinging black robe, and her slider was wound around her left arm. Her face was bleak. He said, "Do you have any messages for Ced Cullen, if I find him?"

"I have no messages for anyone."

"All right. Thanks for the hospitality, Seena. It was good to see you again."

"The next time I see you," she said, "you won't know who I am. Or who you are."

"Perhaps."

He left her and went to the nildoror. Srin'gahar silently accepted the burden of him. Seena stood on the veranda of the station, watching them move away. She did not wave, nor did he. In a little while he could no longer see her. The procession moved out along the bank of the river, past the place where Kurtz had danced all night with the nildoror so many years ago.

Kurtz. Closing his eyes, Gundersen saw the glassy blind stare, the lofty forehead, the flattened face, the wasted flesh, the twisted legs, the deformed feet. Against that he placed his memories of the old Kurtz, that graceful and extraordinary-looking man, so tall and slender, so self-contained. What demons had driven Kurtz, in the end, to surrender his body and his soul to the priests of rebirth? How long had the reshaping of Kurtz taken, and had he felt any pain during the process, and how much awareness did he now have of his own condition? What had Kurtz said? I am Kurtz who toyed with your souls, and now I offer you my own? Gundersen had never heard Kurtz speak in any tone but that of sardonic detachment; how could Kurtz have displayed real emotion, fear, remorse, guilt? I am Kurtz the sinner, take me and deal with me as you wish. I am Kurtz the fallen. I am Kurtz the damned. I am Kurtz, and I am yours. Gundersen imagined Kurtz lying in some misty northern valley, his bones softened by the elixirs of the sulidoror, his body dissolving, becoming a pink jellied lump which now was free to seek a new form, to strive toward an altered kurtzness that would be cleansed of its old satanic impurities. Was it presumptuous to place himself in the same class as Kurtz, to claim the same spiritual shortcomings, to go forward to meet that same terrible destiny? Was Seena not right, that this was a game, that he was merely playing at masochistic self-dramatization, electing himself the hero of a tragic myth, burdened by the obsession to undertake an alien pilgrimage? But the compulsion seemed real enough to him, and not at all a pretense. I will go, Gundersen told himself. I am not Kurtz, but I will go, because I must go. In the distance, receding but yet powerful, the roar and throb of the waterfall still sounded, and as the rushing water hurtled down the face of the cliff it seemed to drum forth the words of Kurtz, the warning, the blessing, the threat, the prophecy, the curse: *water sleep death save sleep sleep fire love water dream cold sleep plan rise fall rise fall rise rise rise.*

Fall.

Twelve

FOR ADMINISTRATIVE PURPOSES, the Earthmen during their years of occupation of Holman's World had marked off boundaries arbitrarily here and here and here, choosing this parallel of latitude, that meridian of longitude, to encompass a district or sector. Since Belzagor itself knew nothing of parallels of latitude nor of other human measures and boundaries, those demarcations by now existed only in the archives of the Company and in the memories of the dwindling human population of the planet. But one boundary was far from arbitrary, and its power still held: the natural line dividing the tropics from the mist country. On one side of that line lay the tropical highlands, sunbathed, fertile, forming the upper limit of the central band of lush vegetation that stretched down to the torrid equatorial jungle. On the other side of that line, only a few kilometers away, the clouds of the north came rolling in, creating the white world of the mists. The transition was sharp and, for a newcomer, even terrifying. One could explain it prosaically enough in terms of Belzagor's axial tilt and the effect that had on the melting of polar snows; one could speak learnedly of the huge icecaps in which so much moisture was locked, icecaps that extended so far into the temperate zones of the planet that the warmth of the tropics was able to nibble at them, liberating great masses of water-vapor that swirled upward, curved pole-ward, and returned to the icecaps as regenerating snow; one could talk of the clash of climates and of the resulting marginal zones that were neither hot nor cold, and forever shrouded in the dense clouds born of that clash. But even these explanations did not prepare one for the initial shock of crossing the divide. One had a few hints: stray tufts of fog that drifted across the boundary and blotted out broad patches of the tropical highlands until the midday sun burned them away. Yet the actual change, when it came, was so profound, so absolute, that it stunned the spirit. On other worlds one grew accustomed to an easy transition from climate to climate, or else to an unvarying global climate; one could not easily accept the swiftness of the descent from warmth and ease to chill and bleakness that came here.

Gundersen and his nildoror companions were still some kilometers short of that point of change when a party of sulidoror came out of the bush and stopped them. They were border guards, he knew. There was no formal guard system, nor any other kind of governmental or quasi-governmental organization; but sulidoror nevertheless patrolled the border and interrogated those who wished to cross it. Even in the time of the Company the jurisdiction of the sulidoror had been respected, after a fashion: it might have cost too much effort to override it, and so the few Earthmen bound for the mist-country stations obligingly halted and stated their destinations before going on.

Gundersen took no part in the discussion. The nildoror and the sulidoror drew to one side, leaving him alone to contemplate the lofty banks of white mist on the northern horizon. There seemed to be trouble. One tall, sleek young sulidor pointed several times at Gundersen and spoke at length; Srin'gahar replied in a few syllables, and the sulidor appeared to grow angry, striding back and forth and vehemently knocking bark from trees with swipes of his huge claws. Srin'gahar spoke again, and then some agreement was reached; the angry sulidor stalked off into the forest and Srin'gahar beckoned to Gundersen to remount. Guided by the two sulidoror who remained, they resumed the northward march.

"What was the argument about?" Gundersen asked.

"Nothing."

"But he seemed very angry."

"It did not matter," said Srin'gahar.

"Was he trying to keep me from crossing the boundary?"

"He felt you should not go across," Srin'gahar admitted.

"Why? I have a many-born's permission."

"This was a personal grudge, friend of my journey. The sulidor claimed that you had offended him in time past. He knew you from the old days."

"That's impossible," Gundersen said. "I had hardly any contact at all with sulidoror back then. They never came out of the mist country and I scarcely ever went into it. I doubt that I spoke a dozen words to sulidoror in eight years on this world."

"The sulidor was not wrong in remembering that he had had contact with you," said Srin'gahar gently. "I must tell you that there are reliable witnesses to the event."

"When? Where?"

"It was a long time ago," Srin'gahar said. The nildor appeared content with that vague answer, for he offered no other details. After a few moments of silence he added, "The sulidor had good reason to be unhappy with you, I think. But we told him that you meant to atone for all of your past deeds, and in the end he yielded. The sulidoror often are a stubborn and vindictive race."

"What did I *do* to him?" Gundersen demanded.

"We do not need to talk of such things," replied Srin'gahar.

Since the nildor then retreated into impermeable silence, Gundersen had ample time to ponder the grammatical ambiguities of that last sentence. On the basis of its verbal content alone, it might have meant "It is useless to talk of such things," or "It would be embarrassing to me to talk of such things," or "It is improper to talk of such things," or "It is tasteless to talk of such things." Only with the aid of the supplementary gestures, the movements of the crest-spines, the trunk, the ears, could the precise meaning be fathomed, and Gundersen had neither the skill nor the right position for detecting those gestures. He was puzzled, for he had no recollection of ever having given offense to a sulidor, and could not comprehend how he might have done it even indirectly or unknowingly; but after a while he concluded that Srin'gahar was deliberately being cryptic, and might be speaking in parables too subtle or too alien for an Earthman's mind to catch. In any case the sulidor had withdrawn his mysterious objections to Gundersen's journey, and the mist country was only a short distance away. Already the foliage of the jungle trees was more sparse than it had been a kilometer or two back, and the trees themselves were smaller and more widely spaced. Pockets of heavy fog now were more frequent. In many places the sandy yellow soil was wholly exposed. Yet the air was warm and clear and the underbrush profuse, and the bright golden sun was reassuringly visible; this was still unmistakably a place of benign and even commonplace climate.

Abruptly Gundersen felt a cold wind out of the north, signaling change. The path wound down a slight incline, and when it rose on the far side he looked over a hummock into a broad field of complete desolation, a no-thing's-land between the jungle and the mist country. No tree, no shrub, no moss grew here; there was only the yellow soil, covered with a sprinkling of pebbles. Beyond this sterile zone Gundersen was confronted by a white palisade fiercely glittering with reflected sunlight; seemingly it was a cliff of ice hundreds of meters high that barred the way as far as he could see. In the extreme distance, behind and above this white wall, soared the tip of a high-looming mountain, pale red in color, whose rugged spires and peaks and parapets stood forth sharply and strangely against an iron-gray sky. Everything appeared larger than life, massive, monstrous, excessive.

"Here you must walk by yourself," said Srin'gahar. "I regret this, but it is the custom. I can carry you no farther."

Gundersen clambered down. He was not unhappy about the change; he felt that he should go to rebirth under his own power, and he had grown abashed at sitting astride Srin'gahar for so many hundreds of kilometers. But unexpectedly he found himself panting after no more than fifty meters of walking beside the five nildoror. Their pace was slow and stately, but the air here, evidently, was thinner than he knew. He forced himself to hide his distress. He would go on. He felt light-headed, oddly buoyant, and he would master the pounding in his chest and the throbbing in his temples. The new chill in the air was invigorating in its austerity. They were halfway across the zone of emptiness, and Gundersen now could clearly tell that what had appeared to be a solid white barrier stretching across the world was in fact a dense wall of mist at ground level. Outlying strands of that mist kissed his face. At its clammy touch images of death stirred in his mind, skulls and tombs and coffins and veils, but they did not dismay him. He looked toward the rose-red mountain dominating the land far to the north, and as he did so the clouds that lay over the mist country parted, permitting the sun to strike the mountain's highest peak, a snowy dome of great expanse, and it seemed to him then that the face of Kurtz, transfigured, serene, looked down at him out of that smooth rounded peak.

From the whiteness ahead emerged the figure of a giant old sulidor: Na-sinisul, keeping the promise he had made to be their guide. The sulidoror who had accompanied them this far exchanged a few words with Na-sinisul and trudged off back toward the jungle belt. Na-sinisul gestured. Walking alongside Srin'gahar, Gundersen went forward.

In a few minutes the procession entered the mist.

He did not find the mist so solid once he was within it. Much of the time he could see for twenty or thirty or even fifty meters in any direction. There were occasional inexplicable vortices of fog that were much thicker in texture, and in which he could barely make out the green bulk of Srin'gahar beside him, but these were few and quickly traversed. The sky was gray and sunless; at moments the solar ball could be discerned as a vague glow behind the clouds. The landscape was one of raw rock, bare soil, and low trees—practically a tundra, although the air was merely chilly and not really cold. Many of the trees were of species also found in the south, but here they were dwarfed and distorted, sometimes not having the form of trees at all, but running along the ground like woody vines. Those trees that stood upright were no taller than Gundersen, and gray moss draped every branch. Beads of moisture dotted their leaves, their stems, the outcroppings of rock, and everything else.

No one spoke. They marched for perhaps an hour, until

Gundersen's back was bowed and his feet were numb. The ground sloped imperceptibly upward; the air seemed to grow steadily thinner; the temperature dropped quite sharply as the day neared its end. The dreary envelope of low-lying fog, endless and all-engulfing, exacted a toll on Gundersen's spirit. When he had seen that band of mist from outside, glittering brilliantly in the sunlight, it had stirred and excited him, but now that he was inside it he felt small cheer. All color and warmth had drained from the universe. He could not even see the glorious rose-red mountain from here.

Like a mechanical man, he went onward, sometimes even forcing himself into a trot to keep up with the others. Nasinisul set a formidable pace, which the nildoror had no difficulty in meeting, but which pushed Gundersen to his limits. He was shamed by the loudness of his own gasps and grunts, though no one else took notice of them. His breath hung before his face, fog within fog. He wanted desperately to rest. He could not bring himself to ask the others to halt a while and wait for him, though. This was their pilgrimage; he was merely the self-invited guest.

A dismal dusk began to descend. The grayness grew more gray, and the faint hint of sunlight that had been evident now diminished. Visibility lessened immensely. The air became quite cold. Gundersen, dressed for jungle country, shivered. Something that had never seemed important to him before now suddenly perturbed him: the alienness of the atmosphere. Belzagor's air, not only in the mist country but in all regions, was not quite the Eathnorm mix, for there was a trifle too much nitrogen and just a slight deficiency in oxygen; and the residual impurities were different as well. But only a highly sensitive olfactory system would notice anything amiss. Gundersen, conditioned to Belzagor's air by his years of service here, had had no awareness of a difference. Now he did. His nostrils reported a sinister metallic tang; the back of his throat, he believed, was coated with some dark grime. He knew it was a foolish illusion born of fatigue. Yet for a few minutes he found himself trying to reduce his intake of breath, as though it was safest to let as little of the dangerous stuff as possible into his lungs.

He did not stop fretting over the atmosphere and other

discomforts until the moment when he realized he was alone.

The nildoror were nowhere to be seen. Neither was Nasinisul. Mist engulfed everything. Stunned, Gundersen rolled back the screen of his memory and saw that he must have been separated from his companions for several minutes, without regarding it as in any way remarkable. By now they might be far ahead of him on some other road.

He did not call out.

He yielded first to the irresistible and dropped to his knees to rest. Squatting, he pressed his hands to his face, then put his knuckles to the cold ground and let his head loll forward while he sucked in air. It would have been easy to sprawl forward altogether and lose consciousness. They might find him sleeping in the morning. Or frozen in the morning. He struggled to rise, and succeeded on the third attempt.

"Srin'gahar?" he said. He whispered it, making only a private appeal for help.

Dizzy with exhaustion, he rushed forward, stumbling, sliding, colliding with trees, catching his feet in the undergrowth. He saw what was surely a nildor to his left and ran toward it, but when he clutched its flank he found it wet and icy, and he realized that he was grasping a boulder. He flung himself away from it. Just beyond, a file of massive shapes presented themselves: the nildoror marching past him? "Wait?" he called, and ran, and felt the shock at his ankles as he plunged blindly into a shallow frigid rivulet. He fell, landing on hands and knees in the water. Grimly he crawled to the far bank and lay there, recognizing the dark blurred shapes now as those of low, broad trees whipped by a rising wind. All right, he thought. I'm lost. I'll wait right here until morning. He huddled into himself, trying to wring the cold water from his clothes.

The night came, blackness in place of grayness. He sought moons overhead and found none. A terrible thirst consumed him, and he tried to creep back to the brook, but he could not even find that. His fingers were numb; his lips were cracking. But he discovered an island of calm within his discomfort and fear, and clung to it, telling himself that none of what was happening was truly perilous and that all of it was somehow necessary.

Unknown hours later, Srin'gahar and Na-sinisul came to him.

First Gundersen felt the soft probing touch of Srin'gahar's trunk against his cheek. He recoiled and flattened himself on the ground, relaxing slowly as he realized what it was that had brushed his skin. Far above, the nildor said, "Here he is."

"Alive?" Na-sinisul asked, dark voice coming from worlds away, swaddled in layers of fog.

"Alive. Wet and cold. Edmundgundersen, can you stand up?"

"Yes. I'm all right, I think." Shame flooded his spirit. "Have you been looking for me all this time?"

"No," said Na-sinisul blandly. "We continued on to the village. There we discussed your absence. We could not be sure if you were lost or had separated yourself from us with a purpose. And then Srin'gahar and I returned. Did you intend to leave us?"

"I got lost," Gundersen said miserably.

Even now he was not permitted to ride the nildor. He staggered along between Srin'gahar and Na-sinisul, now and then clutching the sulidor's thick fur or grasping the nildor's smooth haunch, steadying himself whenever he felt his strength leaving him or whenever the unseen footing grew difficult. In time lights glimmered in the dark, a pale lantern glow coming milkily through the fogbound backness. Dimly Gundersen saw the shabby huts of a sulidor village. Without waiting for an invitation he lurched into the nearest of the ramshackle log structures. It was steep-walled, musty-smelling, with strings of dried flowers and the bunched skins of animals suspended from the rafters. Several seated sulidoror looked at him with no show of interest. Gundersen warmed himself and dried his clothing; someone brought him a bowl of sweet, thick broth, and a little while afterward he was offered some strips of dried meat, which were difficult to bite and chew but extraordinarily well flavored. Dozens of sulidoror came and went. Once, when the flap of hide covering the door was left open, he caught sight of his nildoror sitting just outside the hut. A tiny fierce-faced animal, fog-white and wizened, skittered up to him and inspected him with disdain: some northern beast, he supposed, that the sulidoror favored as pets. The creature plucked at Gundersen's still soggy clothing and made a cackling sound. Its tufted ears twitched; its sharp little fingers probed his sleeve; its long prehensile tail curled and uncurled. Then it leaped into Gundersen's lap, seized his arm with quick claws, and nipped his flesh. The bite was no more painful than the pricking of a mosquito, but Gundersen wondered what hideous alien infection he would now contract. He made no move to push the little animal away, however. Suddenly a great sulidor paw descended, claws retracted, and knocked the beast across the room with a sweeping swing. The massive form of Na-sinisul lowered itself into a crouch next to Gundersen; the ejected animal chattered its rage from a far corner.

Na-sinisul said, "Did the munzor bite you?"

"Not deeply. Is it dangerous?"

"No harm will come to you," said the sulidor. "We will punish the animal."

"I hope you won't. It was only playing."

"It must learn that guests are sacred," said Na-sinisul firmly. He leaned close. Gundersen was aware of the sulidor's fishy breath. Huge fangs gaped in the deep-muzzled mouth. Quietly Na-sinisul said, "This village will house you until you are ready to go on. I must leave with the nildoror, and continue to the mountain of rebirth."

"Is that the big red mountain north of here?"

"Yes. Their time is very close, and so is mine. I will see them through their rebirths, and then my turn will come."

"Sulidoror undergo rebirth too, then?"

Na-sinisul seemed surprised. "How else could it be?"

"I don't know. I know so little about all of this."

"If sulidoror were not reborn," said Na-sinisul, "then nildoror could not be reborn. One is inseparable from the other."

"In what way?"

"If there were no day, could there be night?"

That was too cryptic. Gundersen attempted to press for an explanation, but Na-sinisul had come to speak of other matters. Avoiding the Earthman's questions, the sulidor said, "They tell me that you have come to our country to speak with a man of your own people, the man Cullen. Is that so?"

"It is. It's one of the reasons I'm here, anyway."

"The man Cullen lives three villages north of here, and one village to the west. He has been informed that you have arrived, and he summons you. Sulidoror of this village will conduct you to him when you wish to leave."

"I'll leave in the morning," Gundersen said.

"I must declare one thing to you first. The man Cullen has taken refuge among us, and so he is sacred. There can be no hope of removing him from our country and delivering him to the nildoror."

"I ask only to speak with him."

"That may be done. But your treaty with the nildoror is known to us. You must remember that you can fulfill that treaty only by a breach of our hospitality."

Gundersen made no reply. He did not see how he could promise anything of this nature to Na-sinisul without at the same time forswearing his promise to the many-born Vol'himyor. So he clung to his original inner treaty: he would speak with Cedric Cullen, and then he would decide how to act. But it distrubed him that the sulidoror were already aware of his true purpose in seeking Cullen.

Na-sinisul left him. Gundersen attempted to sleep, and for a while he achieved an uneasy doze. But the lamps flickered all night in the sulidor hut, and lofty sulidoror strode back and forth noisily around and about him, and the nildoror just outside the building engaged in a long debate of which Gundersen could catch only a few meaningless syllables. Once Gundersen awoke to find the little long-eared munzor sitting on his chest and cackling. Later in the night three sulidoror hacked up a bloody carcass just next to the place where Gundersen huddled. The sounds of the rending of flesh awakened him briefly, but he slipped back into his troubled sleep, only to wake again when a savage quarrel erupted over the division of the meat. When the bleak gray dawn came, Gundersen felt more tired than if he had not slept at all.

He was given breakfast. Two young sulidoror, Se-holomir and Yi-gartigok, announced that they had been chosen to escort him to the village where Cullen was staying. Na-sinisul and the five nildoror prepared to leave for the mountain of rebirth. Gundersen made his farewells to his traveling companions.

"I wish you joy of your rebirth," he said, and watched as the huge shapes moved off into the mist.

Not long afterward he resumed his own journey. His new guides were taciturn and aloof: just as well, for he wanted no conversation as he struggled through this hostile country. He needed to think. He was not sure at all what he would do after he had seen Cullen; his original plan of undergoing rebirth, which had seemed so noble in the abstract, now struck him as the highest folly—not only because of what Kurtz had become, but because he saw it as a trespass, an unspontaneous and self-conscious venture into the rites of an alien species. Go to the rebirth mountain, yes. Satisfy your curiosity. But submit to rebirth? For the first time he was genuinely unsure whether he would, and more than half suspicious that in the end he would draw back, unreborn.

The tundra of the border zone was giving way now to forest country which seemed a curious inversion to him: trees growing larger here in higher latitudes. But these were different trees. The dwarfed and twisted shrubs to his rear were natives of the jungle, making an unhappy adaptation to the mist; here, deeper in the mist country, true northern trees grew. They were thick-boled and lofty, with dark corrugated bark and tiny sprays of needle-like leaves. Fog shrouded their upper branches. Through this cold and misty forest too there ran lean, straggly animals, long-nosed and bony, which erupted from holes in the ground and sped up the sides of trees, evidently in quest of bough-dwelling rodents and birds. Broad patches of ground were covered with snow here, although summer was supposedly approaching in this hemisphere. On the second night northward there came a hailstorm when a dense and tossing cloud of ice rode toward them on a thin whining wind. Mute and glum, Gundersen's companions marched on through it, and so did he, not enjoying it.

Generally now the mist was light at ground level, and often there was none at all for an hour or more, but it congealed far overhead as an unbroken veil, hiding the sky. Gundersen became accustomed to the barren soil, the angular branches of so many bare trees, the chilly penetrating dampness that was so different from the jungle's humidity. He came to find beauty in the starkness. When fleecy coils of mist drifted like ghosts across a wide gray stream, when furry beasts sprinted over glazed fields of ice, when some hoarse ragged cry broke the incredible stillness, when the marchers turned an angle in the path and came upon a white tableau of harsh wintry emptiness, Gundersen responded with a strange kind of delight. In the mist country, he thought, the hour is always the hour just after dawn, when everything is clean and new.

On the fourth day Se-holomir said, "The village you seek lies behind the next hill."

Thirteen

IT WAS A substantial settlement, forty huts or more arranged in two rows, flanked on one side by a grove of soaring trees and on the other by a broad silvery-surfaced lake. Gundersen approached the village through the trees, with the lake shining beyond. A light fall of snowflakes wandered through the quiet air. The mists were high just now, thickening to an impenetrable ceiling perhaps five hundred meters overhead.

"The man Cullen—?" Gundersen asked.

Cullen lay in a hut beside the lake. Two sulidoror guarded the entrance, stepping aside at a word from Yi-gartigok; two sulidoror more stood at the foot of the pallet of twigs and hides on which Cullen rested. They too stepped aside, revealing a burned-out husk of a man, a remnant, a cinder.

"Are you here to fetch me?" Cullen asked. "Well, Gundy, you're too late."

Cullen's golden hair had turned white and gone coarse; it was a tangled snowy mat through which patches of pale blotched scalp showed. His eyes, once a gentle liquid green, now were muddy and dull, with angry bloodshot streaks in the yellowed whites. His face was a mask of skin over bones, and the skin was flaky and rough. A blanket covered him from the chest down, but the severe emaciation of his arms indicated that the rest of his body probably was similarly eroded. Of the old Cullen little seemed to remain except the mild, pleasant voice and the cheerful smile, now grotesque emerging from the ravaged face. He looked like a man of a hundred years.

"How long have you been this way?" Gundersen demanded.

"Two months. Three, I don't know. Time melts here, Gundy. But there's no going back for me now. This is where I stop. Terminal. Terminal."

Gundersen knelt by the sick man's pallet. "Are you in pain? Can I give you something?"

"No pain," Cullen said. "No drugs. Terminal."

"What do you have?" Gundersen asked, thinking of Dykstra and his woman lying gnawed by alien larvae in a pool of muck, thinking of Kurtz anguished and transformed at Shangri-la Falls, thinking of Seena's tale of Gio' Salamone turned to crystal. "A native disease? Something you picked up around here?"

"Nothing exotic," said Cullen. "I'd guess it's the old inward rot, the ancient enemy. The crab, Gundy. The crab. In the gut. The crab's pincers are in my gut."

"Then you *are* in pain?"

"No," Cullen said. "The crab moves slowly. A nip here, a nip there. Each day there's a little less of me. Some days I feel that there's nothing left of me at all. This is one of the better days."

"Listen," Gundersen said, "I could get you downriver to Seena's place in a week. She's bound to have a medical kit, a space tube of anticarcin for you. You aren't so far gone that we couldn't manage a remission if we act fast, and then we could ship you to Earth for template renewal, and—"

"No. Forget it."

"Don't be absurd! We aren't living in the Middle Ages, Ced. A case of cancer is no reason for a man to lie down in a filthy hut and wait to die. The sulidoror will set up a litter for you. I can arrange it in five minutes. And then—"

"I wouldn't ever reach Seena's, and you know it," Cullen said softly. "The nildoror would pick me up the moment I came out of the mist country. You know that, Gundy. You *have* to know that."

"Well—"

"I don't have the energy to play these games. You're

aware, aren't you, that I'm the most wanted man on this planet?"

"I suppose so."

"Were you sent here to fetch me?"

"The nildoror asked me to bring you back," Gundersen admitted. "I had to agree to it in order to get permission to come up here."

"Of course." Bitterly.

"But I stipulated that I wouldn't bring you out unless you'd come willingly," Gundersen said. "Along with certain other stipulations. Look, Ced, I'm not here as Judas. I'm traveling for reasons of my own, and seeing you is strictly a side-venture. But I want to help you. Let me bring you down to Seena's so you can get the treatment that you have to—"

"I told you," Cullen said, "the nildoror would grab me as soon as they had a chance."

"Even if they knew you were mortally ill and being taken down to the falls for medical care?"

"Especially so. They'd love to save my soul as I lay dying. I won't give them the satisfaction, Gundy. I'm going to stay here, safe, beyond their reach, and wait for the crab to finish with me. It won't be long now. Two days, three, a week, perhaps even tonight. I appreciate your desire to rescue me. But I won't go."

"If I got a promise from the nildoror to let you alone until you were able to undergo treat—"

"I won't go. You'd have to force me. And that's outside the scope of your promise to the nildoror, isn't it?" Cullen smiled for the first time in some minutes. "There's a flask of wine in the corner there. Be a good fellow."

Gundersen went to get it. He had to walk around several sulidoror. His colloquy with Cullen had been so intense, so private, that he had quite forgotten that the hut was full of sulidoror: his two guides, Cullen's guards, and at least half a dozen others. He picked up the wine and carried it to the pallet. Cullen, his hand trembling, nevertheless managed not to spill any. When he had had his fill, he offered the flask to Gundersen, asking him so insistently to drink that Gundersen could not help but accept. The wine was warm and sweet.

"Is it agreed," Cullen said, "that you won't make any

attempt to take me out of this village? I know you wouldn't seriously consider handing me over to the nildoror. But you might decide to get me out of here for the sake of saving my life. Don't do that either, because the effect would be the same: the nildoror would get me. I stay here. Agreed?"

Gundersen was silent a while. "Agreed," he said finally.

Cullen looked relieved. He lay back, face toward the wall, and said, "I wish you hadn't wasted so much of my energy on that one point. We have so much more to talk about. And now I don't have the strength."

"I'll come back later. Rest, now."

"No. Stay here. Talk to me. Tell me where you've been all these years, why you came back here, who you've seen, what you've done. Give me the whole story. I'll rest while I'm listening. And afterward—and afterward—"

Cullen's voice faded. It seemed to Gundersen that he had slipped into unconsciousness, or perhaps merely sleep. Cullen's eyes were closed; his breath was slow and labored. Gundersen remained silent. He paced the hut uneasily, studying the hides tacked to the walls, the crude furniture, the debris of old meals. The sulidoror ignored him. Now there were eight in the hut, keeping their distance from the dying man and yet focusing all their attention on him. Momentarily Gundersen was unnerved by the presence of these giant two-legged beasts, these nightmare creatures with fangs and claws and thick tails and drooping snouts, who came and went and moved about as though he were less than nothing to them. He gulped more wine, though he found the texture and flavor of it unpleasant.

Cullen said, eyes still shut, "I'm waiting. Tell me things."

Gundersen began to speak. He spoke of his eight years on Earth, collapsing them into six curt sentences. He spoke of the restlessness that had come over him on Earth, of his cloudy and mystifying compulsion to return to Belzagor, of the sense of a need to find a new structure for his life now that he had lost the scaffolding that the Company had been for him. He spoke of his journey through the forest to the lakeside encampment, and of how he had danced among the nildoror, and how they had wrung from him the qualified promise to bring them Cullen. He spoke of Dykstra and his woman in their forest ruin, editing the tale somewhat in respect for Cullen's own condition, though he suspected that such charity was unnecessary. He spoke of being with Seena again on the Night of the Five Moons. He spoke of Kurtz and how he had been changed through rebirth. He spoke of his pilgrimage into the mist country.

He was certain at least three times that Cullen had fallen asleep, and once he thought that the sick man's breathing had ceased altogether. Each time Gundersen paused, though, Cullen gave some faint indication—a twitch of the mouth, a flick of the fingertips—that he should go on. At the end, when Gundersen had nothing left to say, he stood in silence a long while waiting for some new sign from Cullen, and at last, faintly, Cullen said, "Then?"

"Then I came here."

"And where do you go after here?"

"To the mountain of rebirth," said Gundersen quietly.

Cullen's eyes opened. With a nod he asked that his pillows be propped up, and he sat forward, locking his fingers into his coverlet. "Why do you want to go there?" he asked.

"To find out what kind of thing rebirth is."

"You saw Kurtz?"

"Yes."

"He also wanted to learn more about rebirth," Cullen said. "He already understood the mechanics of it, but he had to know its inwardness as well. To try it for himself. It wasn't just curiosity, of course. Kurtz had spiritual troubles. He was courting self-immolation because he'd persuaded himself he needed to atone for his whole life. Quite true, too. Quite true. So he went for rebirth. The sulidoror obliged him. Well, behold the man. I saw him just before I came north."

"For a while I thought I might try rebirth also," said Gundersen, caught unawares by the words surfacing in his mind. "For the same reasons. The mixture of curiosity and guilt. But I think I've given the idea up now. I'll go to the mountain to see what they do, but I doubt that I'll ask them to do it to me."

"Because of the way Kurtz looks?"

"Partly. And also because my original plan looks too—

well, too *willed.* Too unspontaneous. An intellectual choice, not an act of faith. You can't just go up there and volunteer for rebirth in a coldly scientific way. You have to be driven to it."

"As Kurtz was?" Cullen asked.

"Exactly."

"And as you aren't?"

"I don't know any longer," Gundersen said. "I thought I was driven, too. I told Seena I was. But somehow, now that I'm so close to the mountain, the whole quest has started to seem artificial to me.

"You're sure you aren't just afraid to go through with it?"

Gundersen shrugged. "Kurtz wasn't a pretty sight."

"There are good rebirths and bad rebirths," Cullen said. "He had a bad rebirth. How it turns out depends on the quality of one's soul, I gather, and on a lot of other things. Give us some more wine, will you?"

Gundersen extended the flask. Cullen, who appeared to be gaining strength, drank deeply.

"Have you been through rebirth?" Gundersen asked.

"Me? Never. Never even tempted. But I know a good deal about it. Kurtz wasn't the first of us to try it, of course. At least a dozen went before him."

"Who?"

Cullen mentioned some names. They were Company men, all of them from the list of those who had died while on field duty. Gundersen had known some of them; others were figures out of the far past, before he or Cullen had ever come to Holman's World.

Cullen said, "And there were others. Kurtz looked them up in the records, and the nildoror gave him the rest of the story. None of them ever returned from the mist country. Four or five of them turned out like Kurtz—transformed into monsters."

"And the others?"

"Into archangels, I suppose. The nildoror were vague about it. Some sort of transcendental merging with the universe, an evolution to the next bodily level, a sublime ascent—that kind of thing. All that's certain is that they never came back to Company territory. Kurtz was hoping on an outcome like that. But unfortunately Kurtz was Kurtz, half angel and half demon, and that's how he was reborn. And that's what Seena nurses. In a way it's a pity you've lost your urge, Gundy. You might just turn out to have one of the good rebirths. Can you call Hor-tenebor over? I think I should have some fresh air, if we're going to talk so much. He's the sulidor leaning against the wall there. The one who looks after me, who hauls my old bones around. He'll carry me outside."

"It was snowing a little while ago, Ced."

"So much the better. Shouldn't a dying man see some snow? This is the most beautiful place in the universe," Cullen said. "Right here, in front of this hut. I want to see it. Get me Hor-tenebor."

Gundersen summoned the sulidor. At a word from Cullen, Hor-tenebor scooped the fragile, shrunken invalid into his immense arms and bore him through the door-flap of the hut, setting him down on a cradle-like framework overlooking the lake. Gundersen followed. A heavy mist had descended on the village, concealing even the huts closest at hand, but the lake itself was clearly visible under the gray sky. Fugitive wisps of mist hung just above the lake's dull surface. A bitter chill was in the air, but Cullen, wrapped only in a thin hide, showed no discomfort. He held forth his hand, palm upraised, and watched with the wonder of a child as snowflakes struck it.

At length Gundersen said, "Will you answer a question?"

"If I can."

"What was it you did that got the nildoror so upset?"

"They didn't tell you when they sent you after me?"

"No," Gundersen said. "They said that you would, and that in any case it didn't really matter to them whether I knew or not. Seena didn't know either. And I can't begin to guess. You were never the kind who went in for killing or torturing intelligent species. You couldn't have been playing around with the serpent venom the way Kurtz was—he was doing that for years and they never tried to grab him. So what could you possibly have done that caused so much—"

"The sin of Actaeon," said Cullen.

"Pardon?"

"The sin of Actaeon, which was no sin at all, but really just an accident. In Greek myth he was a huntsman who blundered upon Diana bathing, and saw what he shouldn't have seen. She changed him into a stag and he was torn to pieces by his own hounds."

"I don't understand what that has to do with—"

Cullen drew a long breath. "Did you ever go up on the central plateau?" he asked, his voice low but firm. "Yes. Yes, of course you did. I remember, you crash-landed there, you and Seena, on your way back to Fire Point after a holiday on the coast, and you were stranded a little while and weird animals bothered you and that was when Seena first started to hate the plateau. Right? Then you know what a strange and somehow mysterious place it is, a place apart from the rest of this planet, where not even the nildoror like to go. All right. I started to go there, a year or two after relinquishment. It became my private retreat. The animals of the plateau interested me, the insects, the plants, everything. Even the air had a special taste—sweet, clean. Before relinquishment, you know, it would have been considered a little eccentric for anybody to visit the plateau on his free time, or at any other time. Afterward nothing mattered to anyone. The world was mine. I made a few plateau trips. I collected specimens. I brought some little oddities to Seena, and she got to be fond of them before she realized they were from the plateau, and little by little I helped her overcome her irrational fear of the plateau. Seena and I went there often together, sometimes with Kurtz also. There's a lot of flora and fauna from the plateau at Shangri-la Station; maybe you noticed it. Right? We collected all that. The plateau came to seem like any other place to me, nothing supernatural, nothing eerie, merely a neglected backwoods region. And it was my special place, where I went whenever I felt myself growing empty or bored or stale. A year ago, maybe a little less than a year, I went into the plateau. Kurtz had just come back from his rebirth, and Seena was terribly depressed by what had happened to him, and I wanted to get her a gift, some animal, to cheer her up. This time I came down a little to the southwest of my usual landing zone, over in a part of the plateau I had never seen before, where two rivers meet. One of the first things I noticed was how ripped up the shrubbery was. Nildoror! Plenty nildoror! An immense area had been grazed, and you know how nildoror graze. It made me curious. Once in a while I had seen an isolated nildor on the plateau, always at a distance, but never a whole herd. So I followed the line of devastation. On and on it went, this scar through the forest, with broken branches and trampled underbrush, all the usual signs. Night came, and I camped, and it seemed to me I heard drums in the night. Which was foolish, since nildoror don't use drums; I realized after a while that I heard them dancing, pounding the ground, and these were reverberations carried through the soil. There were other sounds, too: screams, bellows, the cries of frightened animals. I had to know what was happening. So I broke camp in the middle of the night and crept through the jungle, hearing the noise grow louder and louder, until finally I reached the edge of the trees, where the jungle gave way to a kind of broad savanna running down to the river, and there in the open were maybe five hundred nildoror. Three moons were up, and I had no trouble seeing. Gundy, would you believe that they had *painted* themselves? Like savages, like something out of a nightmare. There were three deep pits in the middle of the clearing. One of the pits was filled with a kind of wet red mud, and the other two contained branches and berries and leaves that the nildoror had trampled to release dark pigments, one black, one blue. And I watched the nildoror going down to these pits, and first they'd roll in the pit of red mud and come up plastered with it, absolutely scarlet; and then they'd go to the adjoining pits and give each other dark stripes over the red, hosing it on with their trunks. A barbaric sight: all that color, all that flesh. When they were properly decorated, they'd go running—not strolling, *running*—across the field to the place of dancing, and they'd begin that four-step routine. You know it: boom boom *boom* boom. But infinitely more fierce and frightening now, on account of the war-paint. An army of wild-looking nildoror, stamping their feet, nodding their tremendous heads, lifting their trunks, bellowing, stabbing their tusks into the ground, capering, singing, flapping their ears. Frightening, Gundy, frightening. And the moonslight on their painted bodies—

"Keeping well back in the forest, I circled around to the west to get a better view. And saw something on the far side of the dancers that was even stranger than the paint. I saw a corral with log walls, huge, three or four times the size of this village. The nildoror couldn't have built it alone; they might have uprooted trees and hauled them with their trunks, but they must have needed sulidoror to help pile them up and shape them. Inside the corral were plateau animals, hundreds of them, all sizes and shapes. The big leaf-eating ones with giraffe necks, and the kind like rhinos with antlers, and timid ones like gazelles, and dozens that I'd never even seen before, all crowded together as if in a stockyard. There must have been sulidoror hunters out beating the bush for days, driving that menagerie together. The animals were restless and scared. So was I. I crouched in the darkness, waiting, and finally all the nildoror were properly painted, and then a ritual started in the midst of the dancing group. They began to cry out, mostly in their ancient language, the one we can't understand, but also they were talking in ordinary nildororu, and eventually I understood what was going on. Do you know who these painted beasts were? They were sinning nildoror, nildoror who were in disgrace! This was the place of atonement and the festival of purification. Any nildor who had been tinged with corruption in the past year had to come here and be cleansed. Gundy, do you know what sin they had committed? They had taken the venom from Kurtz. The old game, the one everybody used to play down at the serpent station, give the nildoror a swig, take one yourself, let the hallucinations come? These painted prancing nildoror here had all been led astray by Kurtz. Their souls were stained. The Earthman-devil had found their one vulnerable place, the one area of temptation they couldn't resist. So here they were, trying to cleanse themselves. The central plateau is the nildoror purgatory. They don't live there because they need it for their rites, and obviously you don't set up an ordinary encampment in a holy place.

"They danced, Gundy, for hours. But that wasn't the rite of atonement. It was only the prelude to the rite. They danced until I was dizzy from watching them, the red bodies, the dark stripes, the boom of their feet, and then, when no moons were left in the sky, when dawn was near, the real ceremony started. I watched it, and I looked right down into the darkness of the race, into the real nildoror soul. Two old nildoror approached the corral and started kicking down the gate. They broke an opening maybe ten meters wide, and stepped back, and the penned-up animals came rushing out onto the plain. The animals were terrified from all the noise and dancing, and from being imprisoned, and they ran in circles, not knowing what to do or where to go. And the rest of the nildoror charged into them. The peaceful, noble, nonviolent nildoror, you know? Snorting. Trampling. Spearing with their tusks. Lifting animals with their trunks and hurling them into trees. An orgy of slaughter. I became sick, just watching. A nildor can be a terrible machine of death. All that weight, those tusks, the trunk, the big feet—everything berserk, all restraints off. Some of the animals escaped, of course. But most were trapped right in the middle of the chaos. Crushed bodies everywhere, rivers of blood, scavengers coming out of the forest to have dinner while the killing was still going on. That's how the nildoror atone: sin for sin. That's how they purge themselves. The plateau is where they loose their violence, Gundy. They put aside all their restraints and let out the beast that's within them. I've never felt such horror as when I watched how they cleansed their souls. You know how much respect I had for the nildoror. Still have. But to see a thing like that, a massacre, a vision of hell—Gundy, I was numb with despair. The nildoror didn't seem to enjoy the killing, but they weren't hesitant about it, either; they just went on and on, because it had to be done, because this was the form of the ceremony, and they thought nothing more of it than Socrates would think of sacrificing a lamb to Zeus, a cock to Aesculapius. That was the real horror, I think. I watched the nildoror destroying life for the sake of their souls, and it was like dropping through a trapdoor, entering a new world whose existence I had never even suspected, a dark new world beneath the old. Then dawn came. The sun rose, lovely, golden, light glistening on the trampled corpses, and the nildoror were sitting calmly in the midst of the devastation, resting calm, purged, all their inner storms over. It was amazingly peaceful. They had wrestled with their demons, and they had won. They had come through all the night's horror, all the ghastliness, and—I don't know how—they really *were* purged and purified. I can't tell you how to find salvation through violence and destruction. It's alien to me and probably to you. Kurtz knew, though. He took the same road as the nildoror. He fell and fell and fell, through level after level of evil enjoying his corruption, glorying in depravity, and then in the end he was still able to judge himself and find himself wanting, and recoil at the darkness he found inside himself, and so he went and sought rebirth, and showed that the angel within him wasn't altogether dead. This finding of purity by passing through evil—you'll have to come to terms with it by yourself, Gundy. I can't help you. All I can do is tell you of the vision I had at sunrise that morning beside the field of blood. I looked into an abyss. I peered over the edge, and saw where Kurtz had gone, where these nildoror had gone. Where perhaps you'll go. I couldn't follow.

"And then they almost caught me.

"They picked up my scent. While the frenzy was on them, I guess they hadn't noticed—especially with hundreds of animals giving off fear-smells in the corral. But they began to sniff. Trunks started to rise and move around like periscopes. The odor of sacrilege was on the air. The reek of a blaspheming spying Earthman. Five, ten minutes they sniffed, and I stood in the bushes still wrapped in my vision, not even remotely realizing they were sniffing *me*, and suddenly it dawned on me that they knew I was there, and I turned and began to slip away through the forest, and they came after me. Dozens. Can you imagine what it's like to be chased through the jungle by a herd of angry nildoror? But I could fit through places too small for them. I gave them the slip. I ran and ran and ran, until I fell down dizzy in a thicket and vomited, and I rested, and then I heard them bashing along on my trail, and I ran some more. And came to a swamp, and jumped in, hoping they'd lose my scent. And hid in the reeds and marshes, while things I couldn't see nipped at me from below. And the nildoror ringed the entire region. We know you're in there, they called to me. Come out. Come out. We forgive you and we wish to purify you. They explained it quite reasonably to me. I had inadvertently—oh, of course, inadvertently, they were diplomatic!—seen a ceremony that no one but a nildor was allowed to see, and now it would be necessary to wipe what I had seen from my mind, which could be managed by means of a simple technique that they didn't bother to describe to me. A drug, I guess. They invited me to come have part of my mind blotted out. I didn't accept. I didn't say anything. They went right on talking, telling me that they held no malice, that they realized it obviously hadn't been my intention to watch their secret ceremony, but nevertheless since I had seen it they must now take steps, et cetera, et cetera. I began to crawl downstream, breathing through a hollow reed. When I surfaced the nildoror were still calling to me, and now they sounded more angry, as far as it's possible to tell such a thing. They seemed annoyed that I had refused to come out. They didn't blame me for spying on them, but they did object that I wouldn't let them purify me. That was my real crime: not that I hid in the bushes and watched them, but declining afterward to undergo the treatment. That's what they still want me for. I stayed in the creek all day, and when it got dark I slithered out and picked up the vector-beep of my beetle, which turned out to be about half a kilometer away. I expected to find it guarded by nildoror, but it wasn't, and I got in and cleared out fast and landed at Seena's place by midnight. I knew I didn't have much time. The nildoror would be after me from one side of the continent to the other. I told her what had happened, more or less, and I collected some supplies, and I took off for the mist country. The sulidoror would give me sanctuary. They're jealous of their sovereignty; blasphemy or not, I'd be safe here. I came to this village. I explored the mist country a good bit. Then one day I felt the crab in my gut and I knew it was all over. Since then I've been waiting for the end, and the end isn't far away."

He fell silent.

Gundersen, after a pause, said, "But why not risk going back? Whatever the nildoror want to do to you can't be as bad as sitting on the porch of a sulidor hut and dying of cancer."

Cullen made no reply.

''What if they give you a memory-wiping drug?'' Gundersen asked. ''Isn't it better to lose a bit of your past than to lose your whole future? If you'll only come back, Ced, and let us treat your disease—''

''The trouble with you, Gundy, is that you're too logical,'' Cullen said. ''Such a sensible, reasonable, rational chap! There's another flask of wine inside. Would you bring it out?''

Gundersen walked past the crouching sulidoror into the hut, and prowled the musty darkness a few moments, looking for the wine. As he searched, the solution to the Cullen situation presented itself: instead of bringing Cullen to the medicine, he would bring the medicine to Cullen. He would abandon his journey toward the rebirth mountain at least temporarily and go down to Shangri-la Falls to get a dose of anticarcin for him. It might not be too late to check the cancer. Afterward, restored to health, Cullen could face the nildoror or not, as he pleased. What happens between him and the nildoror, Gundersen told himself, will not be a matter that concerns me. I regard my treaty with Vol'himyor as nullified. I said I would bring Cullen forth only with his consent, and clearly he won't go willingly. So my task now is just to save his life. Then I can go to the mountain.

He located the wine and went outside with it.

Cullen leaned backward on the cradle, his chin on his chest, his eyes closed, his breath slow, as if his lengthy monologue had exhausted him. Gundersen did not disturb him. He put the wine down and walked away, strolling for more than an hour, thinking, reaching no conclusion. Then he returned. Cullen had not moved. ''Still asleep?'' Gundersen asked the sulidoror.

''It is the long sleep,'' one of them replied.

Fourteen

THE MIST CAME in close, bringing jewels of frost that hung from every tree, every hut; and by the brink of the leaden lake Gundersen cremated Cullen's wasted body with one long fiery burst of the fusion torch, while sulidoror looked on, silent, solemn. The soil sizzled a while when he was done, and the mist whirled wildly as cold air rushed in to fill the zone of warmth his torch had made. Within the hut were a few unimportant possessions. Gundersen searched through them, hoping to find a journal, a memoir, anything with the imprint of Cedric Cullen's soul and personality. But he found only some rusted tools, and a box of dried insects and lizards, and faded clothing. He left these things where he found them.

The sulidoror brought him a cold dinner. They let him eat undisturbed, sitting on the wooden cradle outside Cullen's hut. Darkness came, and he retreated into the hut to sleep. Se-holomir and Yi-gartigok posted themselves as guards before the entrance, although he had not asked them to stay there. He said nothing to them. Early in the evening he fell asleep.

He dreamed, oddly, not of the newly dead Cullen but of the still living Kurtz. He saw Kurtz trekking through the mist country, the old Kurtz, not yet metamorphosed to his present state: infinitely tall, pale, eyes burning in the domed skull, glowing with strange intelligence. Kurtz carried a pilgrim's staff and strode tirelessly forward into the mist. Accompanying him, yet not really with him, was a procession of nildoror, their green bodies stained bright red by pigmented mud; they halted whenever Kurtz halted, and knelt beside him, and from time to time he let them drink from a tubular canteen he was carrying. Whenever Kurtz offered his canteen to the nildoror, he and not they underwent a transformation. His lips joined in a smooth sealing; his nose lengthened; his eyes, his fingers, his toes, his legs changed and changed again. Fluid, mobile, Kurtz kept no form for long. At one stage in the journey he became a sulidor in all respects but one: his own high-vaulted bald head surmounted the massive hairy body. Then the fur melted from him, the claws shrank, and he took on another form, a lean loping thing, rapacious and swift with double-jointed elbows and long spindly legs. More changes followed. The nildoror sang hymns of adoration, chanting in thick monotonous skeins of gray sound. Kurtz was gracious. He bowed, he smiled, he waved. He passed around his canteen, which never needed replenishing. He rippled through cycle upon cycle of dizzy metamorphosis. From his backpack he drew gifts that he distributed among the nildoror: torches, knives, books, message cubes, computers, statues, color organs, butterflies, flasks of wine, sensors, transport modules, musical instruments, beads, old etchings, holy medallions, baskets of flowers, bombs, flares, shoes, keys, toys, spears. Each gift fetched ecstatic sighs and snorts and moos of gratitude from the nildoror; they frolicked about him, lifting their new treasures in their trunks, excitedly displaying them to one another. "You see?" Kurtz cried. "I am your benefactor. I am your friend. I am the resurrection and the life." They came now to the place of rebirth, not a mountain in Gundersen's dream but rather an abyss, dark and deep, at the rim of which the nildoror gathered and waited. And Kurtz, undergoing so many transformations that his body flickered and shifted from moment to moment, now wearing horns, now covered with scales, now clad in shimmering flame, walked forward while the nildoror cheered him, saying to him, "This is the place, rebirth will be yours," and he stepped into the abyss, which enfolded him in absolute night. And then from the depths of the pit came a single prolonged cry, a shrill wail of terror and dismay so awful that it awakened Gundersen, who lay sweating and shivering for hours waiting for dawn.

In the morning he shouldered his pack and made signs of departing. Se-holomir and Yi-gartigok came to him; and one of the sulidoror said, "Where will you go now?"

"North."

"Shall we go with you?"

"I'll go alone," Gundersen said.

It would be a difficult journey, perhaps a dangerous one, but not impossible. He had direction-finding equipment, food concentrates, a power supply, and other such things. He had the necessary stamina. He knew that the sulidoror villages along the way would extend hospitality to him if he needed it. But he hoped not to need it. He had been escorted long enough, first by Srin'gahar, then by various sulidoror; he felt he should finish this pilgrimage without a guide.

Two hours after sunrise he set out.

It was a good day for beginning such an endeavor. The air was crisp and cool and clear and the mist was high; he could see surprisingly far in all directions. He went through the forest back of the village and emerged on a fair-sized hill from the top of which he was able to gauge the landscape ahead. He saw rugged, heavily forested country, much broken by rivers and streams and lakes; and he succeeded in glimpsing the tip of the mountain of rebirth, a jagged sentinel in the north. That rosy peak on the horizon seemed close enough to grasp. Just reach out; just extend the fingers. And the fissures and hillocks and slopes that separated him from his goal were no challenge; they could be traversed in a few quick bounds. His body was eager for the attempt: heartbeat steady, vision exceptionally keen, legs moving smoothly and tirelessly. He sensed an inward soaring of the soul, a restrained but ecstatic upsweep toward life and power; the phantoms that had veiled him for so many years were dropping away; in this chill zone of mist and snow he felt annealed, purified, tempered, ready to accept whatever must be accepted. A strange energy surged through him. He did not mind the thinness of the air, nor the cold, nor the bleakness of the land. It was a morning of unusual clarity, with bright sunlight cascading through the lofty covering of fog and imparting a dreamlike brilliance to the trees and the bare soil. He walked steadily onward.

The mist closed in at midday. Visibility dwindled until Gundersen could see only eight or ten meters ahead. The giant trees became serious obstacles; their gnarled roots and writhing buttresses now were traps for unwary feet. He picked his way with care. Then he entered a region where large flat-topped boulders jutted at shallow angles from the ground, one after another, slick mist-slippery slabs forming stepping-stones to the land beyond. He had to crawl over them, blindly feeling along, not knowing how much of a drop he was likely to encounter at the far end of each boulder. Jumping off was an act of faith; one of the drops turned out to be about four meters, and he landed hard, so that his ankles tingled for fifteen minutes afterward. Now he felt the first fatigue of the day spreading through his thighs and knees. But yet the mood of controlled ecstasy, sober and nevertheless jubilant, remained with him.

He made a late lunch beside a small, flawlessly circular pond, mirror-bright, rimmed by tall narrow-trunked trees and hemmed in by a tight band of mist. He relished the privacy, the solitude of the place; it was like a spherical room with walls of cotton, within which he was perfectly isolated from a perplexing universe. Here he could shed the tensions of his journey, after so many weeks of traveling with nildoror and sulidoror, worrying all the while that he would give offense in some unknown but unforgivable way. He was reluctant to leave.

As he was gathering his belongings, an unwelcome sound punctured his seclusion: the drone of an engine not far overhead. Shading his eyes against the glare of the mist, he looked up, and after a moment caught a glimpse of an airborne beetle flying just below the cloud-ceiling. The little snubnosed vehicle moved in a tight circle, as if looking for something. For me, he wondered? Automatically he shrank back against a tree to hide, though he knew it was impossible for the pilot to see him here even in the open. A moment later the beetle was gone, vanishing in a bank of fog just to the west. But the magic of the afternoon was shattered. That ugly mechanical droning noise in the sky still reverberated in

Gundersen's mind, shattering his newfound peace.

An hour's march onward, passing through a forest of slender trees with red gummy-looking bark, Gundersen encountered three sulidoror, the first he had seen since parting from Yi-gartigok and Se-holomir that morning. Gundersen was uneasy about the meeting. Would they permit him free access here? These three evidently were a hunting party returning to a nearby village; two of them carried, lashed to a pole slung from shoulder to shoulder, the trussed-up carcass of some large four-legged grazing animal with velvety black skin and long recurved horns. He felt a quick instinctive jolt of fear at the sight of the three gigantic creatures coming toward him among the trees; but to his surprise the fear faded almost as rapidly as it came. The sulidoror, for all their ferocious mien, simply did not hold a threat. True, they could kill him with a slap, but what of that? They had no more reason to attack him than he did to burn them with his torch. And here in their natural surroundings, they did not even seem bestial or savage. Large, yes. Powerful. Mighty of fang and claw. But natural, fitting, proper, and so not terrifying.

"Does the traveler journey well?" asked the lead sulidor, the one who bore no part of the burden of the kill. He spoke in a soft and civil tone, using the language of the nildoror.

"The traveler journeys well," said Gundersen. He improvised a return salutation: "Is the forest kind to the huntsmen?"

"As you see, the huntsmen have fared well. If your path goes toward our village, you are welcome to share our kill this night."

"I go toward the mountain of rebirth."

"Our village lies in that direction. Will you come?"

He accepted the offer, for night was coming on, and a harsh wind was slicing through the trees now. The sulidoror village was a small one, at the foot of a sheer cliff half an hour's walk to the northeast. Gundersen passed a pleasant night there. The villagers were courteous though aloof, in a manner wholly free of any hostility; they gave him a corner of a hut, supplied him with food and drink, and left him alone. He had no sense of being a member of a despised race of ejected conquerors, alien and unwanted. They appeared to look upon him merely as a wayfarer in need of shelter, and showed no concern over his species. He found that refreshing. Of course, the sulidoror did not have the same reasons for resentment as the nildoror, since these forest folk had never actually been turned into slaves by the Company; but he had always imagined a seething, sizzling rage within the sulidoror, and their easygoing kindness now was an agreeable departure from that image, which Gundersen now suspected might merely have been a projection of his own guilts. In the morning they brought him fruits and fish, and then he took his leave.

The second day of his journey alone was not as rewarding as the first. The weather was bad, cold and damp and frequently snowy, with dense mist hanging low nearly all the time. He wasted much of the morning by trapping himself in a cul-de-sac, with a long ridge of hills to his right, another to his left, and, unexpectedly, a broad and uncrossable lake appearing in front of him. Swimming it was unthinkable; he might have to pass several hours in its frigid water, and he would not survive the exposure. So he had to go on a wearying eastward detour over the lesser ridge of hills, which swung him about so that by midday he was in no higher a latitude than he had been the night before. The sight of the fog-wreathed rebirth mountain drew him on, though, and for two hours of the afternoon he had the illusion that he was making up for the morning's delay, only to discover that he was cut off by a swift and vast river flowing from west to east, evidently the one that fed the lake that had blocked him earlier. He did not dare to swim this, either; the current would sweep him into the distant deeps before he had reached the farther bank. Instead he consumed more than an hour following the river upstream, until he came to a place where he might ford it. It was even wider here than below, but its bed looked much more shallow, and some geological upheaval had strewn a line of boulders across it like a necklace, from bank to bank. A dozen of the boulders jutted up, with white water swirling around them; the others, though submerged, were visible just below the surface. Gundersen started across. He was able to hop from the top of one boulder to the next, keeping dry until he had gone nearly a third of the way.

Then he had to scramble in the water, wading shin-deep, slipping and groping. The mist enveloped him. He might have been alone in the universe, with nothing ahead but billows of whiteness, nothing to the rear but the same. He could see no trees, no shore, not even the boulders awaiting him. He concentrated rigidly on keeping his footing and staying to his path. Putting one foot down awry, he slid and toppled, landing in a half-crouch in the river, drenched to the armpits, buffeted by the current, and so dizzied for a moment that he could not rise. All his energy was devoted to clinging to the angular mass of rock beneath him. After a few minutes he found the strength to get to his feet again, and tottered forward, gasping, until he reached a boulder whose upper face stood half a meter above the water; he knelt on it, chilled, soaked, shivering, trying to shake himself dry. Perhaps five minutes passed. With the mist clinging close, he got no drier, but at least he had his breath again, and he resumed his crossing. Experimentally reaching out the tip of a boot, he found another dry-topped boulder just ahead. He went to it. There was still another beyond it. Then came another. It was easy, now: he would make it to the far side without another soaking. His pace quickened, and he traversed another pair of boulders. Then, through a rift in the mist, he was granted a glimpse of the shore.

Something seemed wrong.

The mist sealed itself; but Gundersen hesitated to go on without some assurance that all was as it should be. Carefully he bent low and dipped his left hand in the water. He felt the thrust of the current coming from the right and striking his open palm. Wearily, wondering if cold and fatigue had affected his mind, he worked out the topography of his situation several times and each time came to the same dismaying conclusion: if I am making a northward crossing of a river that flows from west to east, I should feel the current coming from my *left*. Somehow, he realized, he had turned himself around while scrambling for purchase in the water, and since then he had with great diligence been heading back toward the southern bank of the river.

His faith in his own judgment was destroyed. He was tempted to wait here, huddled on this rock, for the mist to clear before going on; but then it occurred to him that he might have to wait through the night, or even longer. He also realized belatedly that he was carrying gear designed to cope with just such problems. Fumbling in his backpack, he pulled out the small cool shaft of his compass and aimed it at the horizon, sweeping his arm in an arc that terminated where the compass emitted its north-indicating beep. It confirmed his conclusions about the current, and he started across the river again, shortly coming to the place of the submerged stepping-stones where he had fallen. This time he had no difficulties.

On the far shore he stripped and dried his clothing and himself with the lowest-power beam of his fusion torch. Night now was upon him. He would not have regretted another invitation to a sulidoror village, but today no hospitable sulidoror appeared. He spent an uncomfortable night huddled under a bush.

The next day was warmer and less misty. Gundersen went warily forward, forever fearing that his hours of hard hiking might be wasted when he came up against some unforeseen new obstacle, but all went well, and he was able to cope with the occasional streams or rivulets that crossed his path. The land here was ridged and folded as though giant hands, one to the north and one to the south, had pushed the globe together; but as Gundersen was going down one slope and up the next, he was also gaining altitude constantly, for the entire continent sloped upward toward the mighty plateau upon which the rebirth mountain was reared.

In early afternoon the prevailing pattern of east-west folds in the land subsided; here the landscape was skewed around so that he found himself walking parallel to a series of gentle north-south furrows, which opened into a wide circular meadow, grassy but treeless. The large animals of the north, whose names Gundersen did not know, grazed here in great numbers, nuzzling in the lightly snow-covered ground. There seemed to be only four or five species—something heavy-legged and humpbacked, like a badly designed cow, and something in the style of an oversized gazelle, and several others—but there were hundreds or even thousands of each kind. Far to the east, at the very border of the plain,

Gundersen saw what appeared to be a small sulidoror hunting-party rounding up some of the animals.

He heard the drone of the engine again.

The beetle he had seen the other day now returned, passing quite low overhead. Instinctively Gundersen threw himself to the ground, hoping to go unnoticed. About him the animals milled uneasily, perplexed at the noise, but they did not bolt. The beetle drifted to a landing about a thousand meters north of him. He decided that Seena must have come after him, hoping to intercept him before he could submit himself to the sulidoror of the mountain of rebirth. But he was wrong. The hatch of the beetle opened, and Van Beneker and his tourists began to emerge.

Gundersen wriggled forward until he was concealed behind a tall stand of thistle-like plants on a low hummock. He could not abide the thought of meeting that crew again, not at this stage in his pilgrimage, when he had been purged of so many vestiges of the Gundersen who had been.

He watched them.

They were walking up to the animals, photographing them, even daring to touch some of the more sluggish beasts. Gundersen heard their voices and their laughter cracking the congealed silence; isolated words drifted randomly toward him, as meaningless as Kurtz's flow of dream-fogged gibberish. He heard, too, Van Beneker's voice cutting through the chatter, describing and explaining and expounding. These nine humans before him on the meadow seemed as alien to Gundersen as the sulidoror. More so, perhaps. He was aware that these last few days of mist and chill, this solitary odyssey through a world of whiteness and quiet, had worked a change in him that he barely comprehended. He felt lean of soul, stripped of the excess baggage of the spirit, a simpler man in all respects, and yet more complex.

He waited an hour or more, still hidden, while the tourist party finished touring the meadow. Then everyone returned to the beetle. Where now? Would Van take them north to spy on the mountain of rebirth? No. No. It wasn't possible. Van Beneker himself dreaded the whole business of rebirth, like any good Earthman; he wouldn't dare to trespass on that mysterious precinct.

When the beetle took off, though, it headed toward the north.

Gundersen, in his distress, shouted to it to turn back. As though heeding him, the gleaming little vehicle veered round as it gained altitude. Van Beneker must have been trying to catch a tailwind, nothing more. Now the beetle made for the south. The tour was over, then. Gundersen saw it pass directly above him and disappear into a lofty bank of fog. Choking with relief, he rushed forward, scattering the puzzled herds with wild loud whoops.

Now all obstacles seemed to be behind him. Gundersen crossed the valley, negotiated a snowy divide without effort, forded a shallow brook, pushed his way through a forest of short, thick, tightly packed trees with narrow pointed crowns. He slipped into an easy rhythm of travel, paying no heed any longer to cold, mist, damp, altitude, or fatigue. He was tuned to his task. When he slept, he slept soundly and well; when he foraged for food to supplement his concentrates, he found that which was good; when he sought to cover distance, he covered it. The peace of the misty forest inspired him to do prodigies. He tested himself, searching for the limits of his endurance, finding them, exceeding them at the next opportunity.

Through this phase of the journey he was wholly alone. Sometimes he saw sulidoror tracks in the thin crust of snow that covered much of the land, but he met no one. The beetle did not return. Even his dreams were empty; the Kurtz phantom that had plagued him earlier was absent now, and he dreamed only blank abstractions, forgotten by the time of awakening.

He did not know how many days had elapsed since the death of Cedric Cullen. Time had flowed and melted in upon itself. He felt no impatience, no weariness, no sense of wanting it all to be over. And so it came as a mild surprise to him when, as he began to ascend a wide, smooth, shelving ledge of stone, about thirty meters wide, bordered by a wall of icicles and decorated in places by tufts of grass and scraggly trees, he looked up and realized that he had commenced the scaling of the mountain of rebirth.

Fifteen

FROM AFAR, the mountain had seemed to rise dramatically from the misty plain in a single sweeping thrust. But now that Gundersen was actually upon its lower slopes, he saw that at close range the mountain dissolved into a series of ramps of pink stone, one atop another. The totality of the mountain was the sum of that series, yet from here he had no sense of a unified bulk. He could not even see the lofty peaks and turrets and domes that he knew must hover thousands of meters above him. A layer of clinging mist severed the mountain less than halfway up, allowing him to see only the broad, incomprehensible base. The rest, which had guided him across hundreds of kilometers, might well have never been.

The ascent was easy. To the right and to the left Gundersen saw sheer faces, impossible spires, fragile bridges of stone linking ledge to ledge; but there was also a switchback path, evidently of natural origin, that gave the patient climber access to the higher reaches. The dung of innumerable nildoror littered this long stone ramp, telling him that he must be on the right route. He could not imagine the huge creatures going up the mountain any other way. Even a sulidor would be taxed by those precipices and gullies.

Chattering munzoror leaped from ledge to ledge, or walked with soft, shuffling steps across terrifying abysses spanned by strands of vines. Goat-like beasts, white with diamond-shaped black markings, capered in graveled pockets of unreachable slopes, and launched booming halloos that echoed through the afternoon. Gundersen climbed steadily. The air was cold but invigorating; the mists were wispy at this level, giving him a clear view before and behind. He looked back and saw the fog-shrouded lowlands suddenly quite far below him. He imagined that he was able to see all the way to the open meadow where the beetle had landed.

He wondered when some sulidor would intercept him.

This was, after all, the most sacred spot on this planet. Were there no guardians? No one to stop him, to question him, to turn him back?

He came to a place about two hours' climb up the mountainside where the upward slope diminished and the ramp became a long horizontal promenade, curving off to the right and vanishing beyond the mass of the mountain. As Gundersen followed it, three sulidoror appeared, coming around the bend. They glanced briefly at him and went past, taking no other notice, as though it were quite ordinary that an Earthman should be going up the mountain of rebirth.

Or, Gundersen thought strangely, as though he were *expected*.

After a while the ramp turned upward again. Now an overhanging stone ledge formed a partial roof for the path, but it was no shelter, for the little cackling wizen-faced munzoror nested up there, dropping pebbles and bits of chaff and worse things down. Monkeys? Rodents? Whatever they were, they introduced a sacrilegious note to the solemnity of this great peak, mocking those who went up. They dangled by their prehensile tails; they twitched their long tufted ears; they spat; they laughed. What were they saying? "Go away, Earthman, this is no shrine of yours!" Was that it? How about, "Abandon hope, all ye who enter here!"

He camped for the night beneath that ledge. Munzoror several times scrambled across his face. Once he woke to what sounded like the sobbing of a woman, deep and intense, in the abyss below. He went to the edge and found a bitter snowstorm raging. Soaring through the storm, rising and sinking, rising and sinking, were sleek bat-like things of the upper reaches, with tubular black bodies and great rubbery yellow wings; they went down until they were lost to his sight, and sped upward again toward their eyries clasping chunks of raw meat in their sharp red beaks. He did not hear the sobbing again. When sleep returned, he lay as if drugged until a brilliant dawn crashed like thunder against the side of the mountain.

He bathed in an ice-rimmed stream that sped down a smooth gully and intersected the path. Then he went upward, and in the third hour of his morning's stint he overtook a party of nildoror plodding toward rebirth. They were not green but pinkish-gray, marking them as members of the kindred race, the nildoror of the eastern hemisphere. Gundersen had never known whether these nildoror enjoyed rebirth facilities in their own continent, or came to undergo the process here. That was answered now. There were five of them, moving slowly and with extreme effort. Their hides were cracked and ridged, and their trunks—thicker and longer than those of western nildoror—drooped limply. It wearied him just to look at them. They had good reason to be tired, though: since nildoror had no way of crossing the ocean, they must have taken the land route, the terrible northeastward journey across the dry bed of the Sea of Dust. Occasionally, during his tour of duty there, Gundersen had seen eastern nildoror dragging themselves through that crystalline wasteland, and at last he understood what their destination had been.

"Joy of your rebirth!" he called to them as he passed, using the terse eastern inflection.

"Peace be on your journey," one of the nildoror replied calmly.

They, too, saw nothing amiss in his presence here. But he did. He could not avoid thinking of himself as an intruder, an interloper. Instinctively he began to lurk and skulk, keeping to the inside of the path as though that made him less conspicuous. He anticipated his rejection at any moment by some custodian of the mountain, stepping forth suddenly to block his climb.

Above him, another two or three spirals of the path overhead, he spied a scene of activity.

Two nildoror and perhaps a dozen sulidoror were in view up there, standing at the entrance to some dark chasm in the mountainside. He could see them only by taking up a precarious position at the rim of the path. A third nildor emerged from the cavern; several sulidoror went in. Some way-station, maybe, on the road to rebirth? He craned his neck to see, but as he continued along his path he reached a point from which that upper level was no longer visible.

It took him longer than he expected to reach it. The switch-back path looped out far to one side in order to encircle a narrow jutting spiky tower of rock sprouting from the great mountain's flank, and the detour proved to be lengthy. It carried Gundersen well around to the northeastern face. By the time he was able to see the level of the chasm again, a sullen twilight was falling, and the place he sought was still some-where above him.

Full darkness came before he was on its level. A heavy blanket of fog sat close upon things now. He was perhaps midway up the peak. Here the path spread into the mountain's face, creating a wide plaza covered with brittle flakes of pale stone, and against the vaulting wall of the mountain Gunder-sen saw a black slash, a huge inverted V, the opening of what must be a mighty cavern. Three nildoror lay sleeping to the left of this entrance, and five sulidoror, to its right, seemed to be conferring.

He hung back, posting himself behind a convenient boulder and allowing himself wary peeps at the mouth of the cavern. The sulidoror went within, and for more than an hour nothing happened. Then he saw them emerge, awaken one of the nildoror, and lead it inside. Another hour passed before they came back for the second. After a while they fetched the third. Now the night was well advanced. The mist, the constant companion here, approached and clung. The big-beaked bat-creatures, like marionettes on strings, swooped down from higher zones of the mountain, shrieking past and vanishing in the drifting fog below, returning moments later in equally swift ascent. Gundersen was alone. This was his moment to peer into the cavern, but he could not bring himself to make the inspection. He hesitated, shivering, unable to go forward. His lungs were choked with mist. He could see nothing in any direction now; even the bat-beasts were invisible, mere dopplering blurts of sound as they rose and fell. He struggled to recapture some of the jauntiness he had felt on that first day after Cullen's death, setting out unaccompanied through this wintry land. With a conscious effort he found a shred of that vigor at last.

He went to the mouth of the cavern.

He saw only darkness within. Neither sulidoror nor nildoror were evident at the entrance. He took a cautious step inward. The cavern was cool, but it was a dry coolness far more agreeable than the mist-sodden chill outside. Drawing his fusion torch, he risked a quick flash of light and discovered that he stood in the center of an immense chamber, the lofty ceiling of which was lost in the shadows overhead. The walls of the chamber were a baroque fantasy of folds and billows and buttresses and fringes and towers, all of stone, polished and translucent, gleaming like convoluted glass during the instant that the light was upon them. Straight ahead, flanked by two rippling wings of stone that were parted like frozen curtains, lay a passageway, wide enough for Gundersen but probably something of a trial for the bulky nildoror who had earlier come this way.

He went toward it.

Two more brief flashes from the torch got him to it. Then he proceeded by touch, gripping one side of the opening and feeling his way into its depths. The corridor bent sharply to the left and, about twenty paces farther on, angled just as sharply the other way. As Gundersen came around the second bend a dim light greeted him. Here a pale green fungoid growth lining the ceiling afforded a minimal sort of illumination. He felt relieved and yet suddenly vulnerable, for, while he now could see, he could also be seen.

The corridor was about twice a nildor's width and three times a nildor's height, rising to the peaked vault in which the fungoids dwelled. It stretched for what seemed an infinite distance into the mountain. Branching off it on both sides, Gundersen saw, were secondary chambers and passages.

He advanced and peered into the nearest of these chambers.

It held something that was large and strange and apparently alive. On the floor of a bare stone cell lay a mass of pink flesh, shapeless and still. Gundersen made out short thick limbs and a tail curled tightly over broad flanks; he could not see its head, nor any distinguishing marks by which he could associate it with a species he knew. It might have been a nildor, but it did not seem quite large enough. As he watched, it swelled with the intake of a breath, and slowly subsided. Many minutes passed before it took another breath. Gundersen moved on.

In the next cell he found a similar sleeping mound of unidentifiable flesh. In the third cell lay another. The fourth cell, on the opposite side of the corridor, contained a nildor of the western species, also in deep slumber. The cell beside it was occupied by a sulidor lying oddly on its back with its limbs poking rigidly upward. The next cell held a sulidor in the same position, but otherwise quite startlingly different, for it had shed its whole thick coat of fur and lay naked, revealing awesome muscles beneath a gray, slick-looking skin. Continuing, Gundersen came to a chamber that housed something even more bizarre: a figure that had a nildor's spines and tusks and trunk but a sulidor's powerful arms and legs and a sulidor's frame. What nightmare composite was this? Gundersen stood awed before it for a long while, trying to comprehend how the head of a nildor might have been joined to the body of a sulidor. He realized that no such joining could have occurred; the sleeper here simply partook of the characteristics of both races in a single body. A hybrid? A genetic mingling?

He did not know. But he knew now that this was no mere way-station on the road toward rebirth. This was the place of rebirth itself.

Far ahead, figures emerged from one of the subsidiary corridors and crossed the main chamber: two sulidoror and a nildor. Gundersen pressed himself against the wall and remained motionless until they were out of sight, disappearing into some distant room. Then he continued inward.

He saw nothing but miracles. He was in a garden of fantasies where no natural barriers held.

Here was a round spongy mass of soft pink flesh with just one recognizable feature sprouting from it: a sulidor's huge tail.

Here was a sulidor, bereft of fur, whose arms were foreshortened and pillar-like, like the limbs of a nildor, and whose body had grown round and heavy and thick.

Here was a sulidor in full fur with a nildor's trunk and ears.

Here was raw meat that was neither nildor nor sulidor, but alive and passive, a mere thing awaiting a sculptor's shaping hand.

Here was another thing that resembled a sulidor whose bones had melted.

Here was still another thing that resembled a nildor who had never had bones.

Here were trunks, spines, tusks, fangs, claws, tails, paws. Here was fur, and here was smooth hide. Here was flesh flowing at will and seeking new shapes. Here were dark chambers, lit only by flickering fungoid-glow, in which no firm distinction of species existed.

Biology's laws seemed suspended here. This was no trifling gene-tickling that he saw, Gundersen knew. On Earth, any skilled helix-parlor technician could redesign an organism's gene-plasm with some cunning thrusts of a needle and a few short spurts of drugs; he could make a camel bring forth a hippopotamus, a cat bring forth a chipmunk, or, for that matter, a woman bring forth a sulidor. One merely enhanced the desired characteristics within sperm and ovum, and suppressed other characteristics, until one had a reasonable facsimile of the creature to be reproduced. The basic genetic building-blocks were the same for every life-form; by rearranging them, one could create any kind of strange and monstrous progeny. But that was not what was being done here.

On Earth, Gundersen knew, it was also possible to persuade any living cell to play the part of a fertilized egg, and divide, and grow, and yield a full organism. The venom from Belzagor was one catalyst for that process; there were others. And so one could induce the stump of a man's arm to regrow that arm; one could scrape a bit of skin from a frog and generate an army of frogs with it; one could even rebuild an entire human being from the shards of his own ruined body. But that was not what was being done here.

What was being done here, Gundersen realized, was a transmutation of species, a change worked not upon ova but upon adult organisms. Now he understood Na-sinisul's remark, when asked if sulidoror also underwent rebirth: "If there were no day, could there be night?" Yes. Nildor into sulidor. Sulidor into nildor. Gundersen shivered in shock. He reeled, clutching at a wall. He was plunged into a universe without fixed points. What was real? What was enduring?

He comprehended now what had happened to Kurtz in this mountain.

Gundersen stumbled into a cell in which a creature lay midway in its metamorphosis. Smaller than a nildor, larger than a sulidor; fangs, not tusks; trunk, not snout; fur, not hide; flat footpads, not claws; body shaped for walking upright.

"Who are you?" Gundersen whispered. "What are you? What were you? Which way are you heading?"

Rebirth. Cycle upon cycle upon cycle. Nildoror bound upon a northward pilgrimage, entering these caves, becoming... sulidoror? Was it possible?

If this is true, Gundersen thought, then we have never really known anything about this planet. And this is true.

He ran wildly from cell to cell, no longer caring whether he might be discovered. Each cell confirmed his guess. He saw nildoror and sulidoror in every stage of metamorphosis, some almost wholly nildoror, some unmistakably sulidoror, but most of them occupying intermediate positions along that journey from pole to pole; more than half were so deep in transformation that it was impossible for him to tell which way they were heading. All slept. Before his eyes flesh flowed, but nothing moved. In these cool shadowy chambers change came as a dream.

Gundersen reached the end of the corridor. He pressed his palms against cold, unyielding stone. Breathless, sweat-drenched, he turned toward the last chamber in the series and plunged into it.

Within was a sulidor not yet asleep, standing over three of the sluggish serpents of the tropics, which moved in gentle coils about him. The sulidor was huge, age-grizzled, a being of unusual presence and dignity.

"Na-sinisul?" Gundersen asked.

"We knew that in time you must come here, Edmund-gundersen."

"I never imagined—I didn't understand—" Gundersen paused, struggling to regain control. More quietly he said, "Forgive me if I have intruded. Have I interrupted your rebirth's beginning?"

"I have several days yet," the sulidor said. "I merely prepare the chamber now."

"And you'll come forth from it as a nildor."

"Yes. Over and over, rebirth after rebirth."

"Life goes in a cycle here, then? Sulidor to nildor to sulidor to nildor to—"

"Yes. Over and over, rebirth after rebirth."

"All nildoror spend part of their lives as sulidoror? All sulidoror spend part of their lives as nildoror?"

"Yes. All."

How had it begun, Gundersen wondered? How had the destinies of these two so different races become entangled? How had an entire species consented to undergo such a metamorphosis? He could not begin to understand it. But he knew now why he had never seen an infant nildor or sulidor. He said, "Are young ones of either race ever born on this world?"

"Only when needed as replacements for those who can be reborn no more. It is not often. Our population is stable."

"Stable, yet constantly changing."

"Through a predictable pattern of change," said Na-sinisul. "When I emerge, I will be Fi'gontor of the ninth birth. My people have waited for thirty turnings for me to rejoin them; but circumstances required me to remain this long in the forest of the mists."

"Is nine rebirths unusual?"

"There are those among us who have been here fifteen times. There are some who wait a hundred turnings to be called once. The summons comes when the summons comes: And for those who merit it, life will have no end."

"No—end—"

"Why should it?" Na-sinisul asked. "In this mountain we are purged of the poisons of age, and elsewhere we purge ourselves of the poisons of sin."

"On the central plateau, that is."

"I see you have spoken with the man Cullen."

"Yes," Gundersen said. "Just before his—death."

"I knew also that his life was over," said Na-sinisul. "We learn things swiftly here."

Gundersen said, "Where are Srin'gahar and Luu'khamin and the others I traveled with?"

"They are here, in cells not far away."

"Already in rebirth?"

"For some days now. They will be sulidoror soon, and will live in the north until they are summoned to assume the nildor form again. Thus we refresh our souls by undertaking new lives."

"During the sulidor phase, you keep a memory of your past life as a nildor?"

"Certainly. How can experience be valuable if it is not retained? We accumulate wisdom. Our grasp of truth is heightened by seeing the universe now through a nildor's eyes, now through a sulidor's. Not in body alone are the two forms different. To undergo rebirth is to enter a new world, not merely a new life."

Hesitantly Gundersen said, "And when someone who is not of this planet undergoes rebirth? What effect is there? What kind of changes happen?"

"You saw Kurtz?"

"I saw Kurtz," said Gundersen. "But I have no idea what Kurtz has become."

"Kurtz has become Kurtz," the sulidor said. "For your kind there can be no true transformation, because you have no complementary species. You change, yes, but you become only what you have the potential to become. You liberate such forces as already exist within you. While he slept, Kurtz chose his new form himself. No one else designed it for him. It is not easy to explain this with words, Edmundgundersen."

"If I underwent rebirth, then, I wouldn't necessarily turn into something like Kurtz?"

"Not unless your soul is as Kurtz's soul, and that is not possible."

"What *would* I become?"

"No one may know these things before the fact. If you wish to discover what rebirth will do to you, you must accept rebirth."

"If I asked for rebirth, would I be permitted to have it?"

"I told you when we first met," said Na-sinisul, "that no one on this world will prevent you from doing anything. You were not stopped as you ascended the mountain of rebirth. You were not stopped when you explored these chambers. Rebirth will not be denied you if you feel you need to experience it.''

Easily, serenely, instantly, Gundersen said, ''Then I ask for rebirth.''

Sixteen

SILENTLY, UNSURPRISED, Na-sinisul leads him to a vacant cell and gestures to him to remove his clothing. Gundersen strips. His fingers fumble only slightly with the snaps and catches. At the sulidor's direction, Gundersen lies on the floor, as all other candidates for rebirth have done. The stone is so cold that he hisses when his bare skin touches it. Na-sinisul goes out. Gundersen looks up at the glowing fungoids in the distant vault of the ceiling. The chamber is large enough to hold a nildor comfortably; to Gundersen, on the floor, it seems immense.

Na-sinisul returns, bearing a bowl made from a hollow log. He offers it to Gundersen. The bowl contains a pale blue fluid. "Drink," says the sulidor softly.

Gundersen drinks.

The taste is sweet, like sugar-water. This is something he has tasted before, and he knows when it was: at the serpent station, years ago. It is the forbidden venom. He drains the bowl, and Na-sinisul leaves him.

Two sulidoror whom Gundersen does not know enter the cell. They kneel on either side of him and begin a low mumbling chant, some sort of ritual. He cannot understand any of it. They knead and stroke his body; their hands, with the fearful claws retracted, are strangely soft, like the pads of a cat. He is tense, but the tension ebbs. He feels the drug taking effect now: a thickness at the back of his head, a tightness in his chest, a blurring of his vision. Na-sinisul is in the room again, although Gundersen did not see him enter. He carries a bowl.

''Drink,'' he says, and Gundersen drinks.

It is another fluid entirely, or perhaps a different distillate of the venom. Its flavor is bitter, with undertastes of smoke and ash. He has to force himself to get to the bottom of the bowl, but Na-sinisul waits, silently insistent, for him to finish it. Again the old sulidor leaves. At the mouth of the cell he turns and says something to Gundersen, but the words are overgrown with heavy blue fur, and will not enter Gundersen's ears. ''What did you say?'' the Earthman asks. ''What? What?'' His own words sprout leaden weights, teardrop-shaped, somber. They fall at once to the floor and shatter. One of the chanting sulidoror sweeps the broken words into a corner with a quick motion of his tail.

Gundersen hears a trickling sound, a glittering spiral of noise, as of water running into his cell. His eyes are closed, but he feels the wetness swirling about him. It is not water, though. It has a more solid texture. A sort of gelatin, perhaps. Lying on his back, he is several centimeters deep in it, and the level is rising. It is cool but not cold, and it insulates him nicely from the chill rock of the floor. He is aware of the faint pink odor of the inflowing gelatin, and of its firm consistency, like the tones of a bassoon in its deepest register. The sulidoror continue to chant. He feels a tube sliding into his mouth, a sleek piccolo-shriek of a tube, and through its narrow core there drips yet another substance, thick, oily, emitting the sound of muted kettledrums as it hits his palate. Now the gelatin has reached the lower curve of his jaw. He welcomes its advance. It laps gently at his chin. The tube is withdrawn from his mouth just as the flow of gelatin covers his lips. ''Will I be able to breathe?'' he asks. A sulidor answers him in cryptic Sumerian phrases, and Gundersen is reassured.

He is wholly sealed in the gelatin. It covers the floor of the chamber to a depth of one meter. Light dimly penetrates it. Gundersen knows that its upper surface is smooth and flawless, forming a perfect seal where it touches the walls of the cell. Now he has become a chrysalis. He will be given nothing more to drink. He will lie here, and he will be reborn.

One must die in order that one may be reborn, he knows.

Death comes to him and enfolds him. Gently he slides into a dark abyss. The embrace of death is tender. Gundersen floats through a realm of trembling emptiness. He hovers suspended in the black void. Bands of scarlet and purple light transfix him, buffeting him like bars of metal. He tumbles. He spins. He soars.

He encounters death once more, and they wrestle, and he is defeated by death, and his body is shivered into splinters, and a shower of bright Gundersen-fragments scatters through space.

The fragments seek one another. They solemnly circle one another. They dance. They unite. They take on the form of Edmund Gundersen, but this new Gundersen glows like pure, transparent glass. He is glistening, a transparent man through whom the light of the great sun at the core of the universe passes without resistance. A spectrum spreads forth from his chest. The brilliance of his body illuminates the galaxies.

Strands of color emanate from him and link him to all who possess *g'rakh* in the universe.

He partakes of the biological wisdom of the cosmos.

He tunes his soul to the essence of what is and what must be.

He is without limits. He can reach out and touch any soul. He reaches toward the soul of Na-sinisul, and the sulidor greets him and admits him. He reaches toward Srin'gahar, toward Vol'himyor the many-born, toward Luu'khamin, Se-holomir, Yi-gartigok, toward the nildoror and sulidoror who lie in the caves of metamorphosis, and toward the dwellers in the misty forests, and toward the dwellers in the steaming jungles, and toward those who dance and rage in the forlorn plateau, and to all others of Belzagor who share in *g'rakh*.

And he comes now to one that is neither nildor nor sulidor, a sleeping soul, a veiled soul, a soul of a color and a timbre and a texture unlike the others. It is an Earthborn soul, the soul of Seena, and he calls softly to her, saying, Awaken, awaken, I love you, I have come for you. She does not awaken. He calls to her, I am new, I am reborn, I overflow with love. Join me. Become part of me. Seena? Seena? Seena? And she does not respond.

He sees the souls of the other Earthmen now. They have *g'rakh,* but rationality is not enough; their souls are blind and silent. Here is Van Beneker; here are the tourists; here are the lonely keepers of solitary outposts in the jungle. Here is the charred gray emptiness where the soul of Cedric Cullen belongs.

He cannot reach any of them.

He moves on, and a new soul gleams beyond the mist. It is the soul of Kurtz. Kurtz comes to him, or he to Kurtz, and Kurtz is not asleep.

Now you are among us, Kurtz says, and Gundersen says, Yes, here I am at last. Soul opens to soul and Gundersen looks down into the darkness that is Kurtz, past the pearl-gray curtain that shrouds his spirit, into a place of terror where black figures shuttle with many legs along ridged webs. Chaotic forms cohere, expand, dissolve within Kurtz. Gundersen looks beyond this dark and dismal zone, and beyond it he finds a cold hard bright light shining whitely out of the deepest place, and then Kurtz says, See? Do you see? Am I a monster? I have goodness within me.

You are not a monster, Gundersen says.

But I have suffered, says Kurtz.

For your sins, Gundersen says.

I have paid for my sins with my suffering, and I should now be released.

You have suffered, Gundersen agrees.

When will my suffering end, then?

Gundersen replies that he does not know, that it is not he who sets the limits of such things.

Kurtz says, I knew you. Nice young fellow, a little slow. Seena speaks highly of you. Sometimes she wishes things had worked out better for you and her. Instead she got me. Here I lie. Here lie we. Why won't you release me?

What can I do, asks Gundersen?

Let me come back to the mountain. Let me finish my rebirth.

Gundersen does not know how to respond, and he seeks

along the circuit of *g'rakh*, consulting Na-sinisul, consulting Vol'himyor, consulting all the many-born ones, and they join, they join, they speak with one voice, they tell Gundersen in a voice of thunder that Kurtz is finished, his rebirth is over, he may not come back to the mountain.

Gundersen repeats this to Kurtz, but Kurtz has already heard. Kurtz shrivels. Kurtz shrinks back into darkness. He becomes enmeshed in his own webs.

Pity me, he calls out to Gundersen across a vast gulf. Pity me, for this is hell, and I am in it.

Gundersen says, I pity you. I pity you. I pity you. I pity you.

The echo of his own voice diminishes to infinity. All is silent. Out of the void, suddenly, comes Kurtz's wordless reply, a shrill and deafening crescendo blast of rage and malevolence, the scream of a flawed Prometheus flailing at the beak that pierces him. The shriek reaches a climax of shattering intensity. It dies away. The shivering fabric of the universe grows still again. A soft violet light appears, absorbing the lingering disharmonies of that one terrible outcry.

Gundersen weeps for Kurtz.

The cosmos streams with shining tears, and on that salty river Gundersen floats, traveling without will, visiting this world and that, drifting among the nebulae, passing through clouds of cosmic dust, soaring over strange suns.

He is not alone. Na-sinisul is with him, and Srin'gahar, and Vol'himyor, and all the others.

He becomes aware of the harmony of all things *g'rakh*. He sees, for the first time, the bonds that bind *g'rakh* to *g'rakh*. He, who lies in rebirth, is in contact with them all, but also they are each in contact with one another, at any time, at every time, every soul on the planet joined in wordless communication.

He sees the unity of all *g'rakh*, and it awes and humbles him.

He perceives the complexity of this double people, the rhythm of its existence, the unending and infinite swing of cycle upon cycle of rebirth and new creation, above all the union, the oneness. He perceives his own monstrous isolation, the walls that cut him off from other men, that cut off man from man, each a prisoner in his own skull. He sees what it is like to live among people who have learned to liberate the prisoner in the skull.

That knowledge dwindles and crushes him. He thinks, We made them slaves, we called them beasts, and all the time they were linked, they spoke in their minds without words, they transmitted the music of the soul one to one to one. We were alone, and they were not, and instead of kneeling before them and begging to share the miracle, we gave them work to do.

Gundersen weeps for Gundersen.

Na-sinisul says, This is no time for sorrow, and Srin'gahar says, The past is past, and Vol'himyor says, Through remorse you are redeemed, and all of them speak with one voice and at one time, and he understands. He understands.

Now Gundersen understands all.

He knows that nildor and sulidor are not two separate species but merely forms of the same creature, no more different than caterpillar and butterfly, though he cannot tell which is the caterpillar, which the butterfly. He is aware of how it was for the nildoror when they were still in their primeval state, when they were born as nildoror and died helplessly as nildoror, perishing when the inevitable decay of their souls came upon them. And he knows the fear and the ecstasy of those first few nildoror who accepted the serpent's temptation and drank the drug of liberation, and became things with fur and claws, misshapen, malformed, transmuted. And he knows their pain as they were driven out, even into the plateau where no being possessing *g'rakh* would venture.

And he knows their sufferings in that plateau.

And he knows the triumph of those first sulidoror, who, surmounting their isolation, returned from the wilderness bearing a new creed. Come and be changed, come and be changed! Give up this flesh for another! Graze no more, but hunt and eat flesh! Be reborn, and live again, and conquer the brooding body that drags the spirit to destruction!

And he sees the nildoror accepting their destiny and giving themselves up joyfully to rebirth, a few, and then more, and then more, and then whole encampments, entire populations, going forth, not to hide in the plateau of purification, but to live in the new way, in the land where mist rules. They cannot resist, because with the change of body comes the blessed liberation of soul, the unity, the bond of *g'rakh* to *g'rakh*.

He understands now how it was for these people when the Earthmen came, the eager, busy, ignorant, pitiful, short-lived Earthmen, who were beings of *g'rakh* yet who could not or would not enter into the oneness, who dabbled with the drug of liberation and did not taste it to the fullest, whose minds were sealed one against the other, whose roads and buildings and pavements spread like pockmarks over the tender land. He sees how little the Earthmen knew, and how little they were capable of learning, and how much was kept from them since they would misunderstand it, and why it was necessary for the sulidoror to hide in the mists of all these years of occupation, giving no clue to the strangers that they might be related to the nildoror, that they were the sons of the nildoror and the fathers of the nildoror as well. For if the Earthmen had known even half the truth they would have recoiled in fright, since their minds are sealed one against the other, and they would not have it any other way, except for the few who dared to learn, and too many of those were dark and demon-ridden, like Kurtz.

He feels vast relief that the time of pretending is over on this world and that nothing need be hidden any longer, that the sulidoror may go down into the lands of the nildoror and move freely about, without fear that the secret and the mystery of rebirth may accidentally be revealed to those who could not withstand such knowledge.

He knows joy that he has come here and survived the test and endured his liberation. His mind is open now, and he has been reborn.

He descends, rejoining his body. He is aware once more that he lies embedded in congealed gelatin on the cold floor of a dark cell abutting a lengthy corridor within a rose-red mountain wreathed in white mist on a strange world. He does not rise. His time is not yet come.

He yields to the tones and colors and odors and textures that flood the universe. He allows them to carry him back, and he floats easily along the time-line, so that now he is a child peering at the shield of night and trying to count the stars, and now he is timidly sipping raw venom with Kurtz and Salamone, and now he enrolls in the Company and tells a personnel computer that his strongest wish is to foster the expansion of the human empire, and now he grasps Seena on a tropic beach under the light of several moons, and now he meets her for the first time, and now he sifts crystals in the Sea of Dust, and now he mounts a nildor, and now he turns his torch on Cedric Cullen, and now he climbs the rebirth mountain, and now he trembles as Kurtz walks into a room, and now he takes the wafer on his tongue, and now he stares at the wonder of a white breast filling his cupped hand, and now he steps forth into mottled alien sunlight, and now he crouches over Henry Dykstra's swollen body, and now, and now, and now, and now....

He hears the tolling of mighty bells.

He feels the planet shuddering and shifting on its axis.

He smells dancing tongues of flame.

He touches the roots of the rebirth mountain.

He feels the souls of nildoror and sulidoror all about him.

He recognizes the words of the hymn the sulidoror sing, and he sings with them.

He grows. He shrinks. He burns. He shivers. He changes.

He awakens.

''Yes,'' says a thick, low voice. ''Come out of it now. The time is here. Sit up. Sit up.''

Gundersen's eyes open. Colors surge through his dazzled brain. It is a moment before he is able to see.

A sulidor stands at the entrance to his cell.

''I am Ti-munilee,'' the sulidor says. ''You are born again.''

''I know you,'' Gundersen says. ''But not by that name. Who are you?''

''Reach out to me and see,'' says the sulidor.

Gundersen reaches out.

''I knew you as the nildor Srin'gahar,'' Gundersen says.

Seventeen

LEANING ON THE sulidor's arm, Gundersen walked unsteadily out of the chamber of rebirth. In the dark corridor he asked, "Have I been changed?"

"Yes, very much," Ti-munilee said.

"How? In what way?"

"You do not know?"

Gundersen held a hand before his eyes. Five fingers, yes, as before. He looked down at his naked body and saw no difference in it. Obscurely he experienced disappointment; perhaps nothing had really happened in that chamber. His legs, his feet, his loins, his belly—everything as it had been.

"I haven't changed at all," he said.

"You have changed greatly," the sulidor replied.

"I see myself, and I see the same body as before."

"Look again," advised Ti-munilee.

In the main corridor Gundersen caught sight of himself dimly reflected in the sleek glassy walls by the light of the glowing fungoids. He drew back, startled. He had changed, yes; he had outkurtzed Kurtz in his rebirth. What peered back at him from the rippling sheen of the walls was scarcely human. Gundersen stared at the mask-like face with hooded slots for eyes, at the slitted nose, the gill-pouches trailing to his shoulders, the many-jointed arms, the row of sensors on the chest, the grasping organs at the hips, the cratered skin, the glow-organs in the cheeks. He looked down again at himself and saw none of those things. Which was the illusion?

He hurried toward daylight.

"Have I changed, or have I not changed?" he asked the sulidor.

"You have changed."

"Where?"

"The changes are within," said the former Srin'gahar.

"And the reflection?"

"Reflections sometimes lie. Look at yourself through my eyes, and see what you are."

Gundersen reached forth again. He saw himself, and it was his old body he saw, and then he flickered and underwent a phase shift and he beheld the being with sensors and slots, and then he was himself again.

"Are you satisfied?" Ti-munilee asked.

"Yes," said Gundersen. He walked slowly toward the lip of the plaza outside the mouth of the cavern. The seasons had changed since he had entered that cavern; now an iron winter was on the land, and the mist was piled deep in the valley, and where it broke he saw the heavy mounds of snow and ice. He felt the presence of nildoror and sulidoror about him, though he saw only Ti-munilee. He was aware of the soul of old Na-sinisul within the mountain, passing through the final phases of a rebirth. He touched the soul of Vol'himyor far to the south. He brushed lightly over the soul of tortured Kurtz. He sensed suddenly, startlingly, other Earthborn souls, as free as his, open to him, hovering nearby.

"Who are you?" he asked.

And they answered, "You are not the first of your kind to come through rebirth intact."

Yes. He remembered. Cullen had said that there had been others, some transformed into monsters, others simply never heard from again.

"Where are you?" he asked them.

They told him, but he did not understand, for what they said was that they had left their bodies behind. "Have I also left my body behind?" he asked. And they said, no, he was still wearing his flesh, for so he had chosen, and they had chosen otherwise. Then they withdrew from him.

"Do you feel the changes?" Ti-munilee asked.

"The changes are within me," said Gundersen.

"Yes. Now you are at peace."

And, surprised by joy, he realized that that was so. The fears, the tensions, were gone. Guilt was gone. Sorrow was gone. Loneliness was gone.

Ti-munilee said, "Do you know who I was, when I was Srin'gahar? Reach toward me."

Gundersen reached. He said, in a moment, "You were one of those seven nildoror whom I would not allow to go to their rebirth, many years ago."

"Yes."

"And yet you carried me on your back all the way to the mist country."

"My time had come again," said Ti-munilee, "and I was happy. I forgave you. Do you remember, when we crossed into the mist country, there was an angry sulidor at the border?"

"Yes," Gundersen said.

"He was another of the seven. He was the one you touched with your torch. He had had his rebirth finally, and still he hated you. Now he no longer does. Tomorrow, when you are ready, reach toward him, and he will forgive you. Will you do that?"

"I will," said Gundersen. "But will he really forgive?"

"You are reborn. Why should he not forgive?" Ti-munilee said. Then the sulidor asked, "Where will you go now?"

"South. To help my people. First to help Kurtz, to guide him through a new rebirth. Then the others. Those who are willing to be opened."

"May I share your journey?"

"You know that answer."

Far off, the dark soul of Kurtz stirred and throbbed. Wait, Gundersen told it. Wait. You will not suffer much longer.

A blast of cold wind struck the mountainside. Sparkling flakes of snow whirled into Gundersen's face. He smiled. He had never felt so free, so light, so young. A vision of a mankind transformed blazed within him. I am the emissary, he thought. I am the bridge over which they shall cross. I am the resurrection and the life. I am the light of the world: he that followeth me shall not walk in darkness, but shall have the light of life. A new commandment I give unto you, that ye love one another.

He said to Ti-munilee, "Shall we go now?"

"I am ready when you are ready."

"Now."

"Now," said the sulidor, and together they began to descend the windswept mountain.

ABOUT THE AUTHOR

ROBERT SILVERBERG was born in New York and makes his home in the San Francisco area. He has written several hundred science fiction stories and over seventy science fiction novels. He has won two Hugo awards and four Nebula awards. He is a past president of the Science Fiction Writers of America. Silverberg's other Bantam titles include *Lord Valentine's Castle*, *Majipoor Chronicles*, *The Book of Skulls*, *The World Inside*, *Thorns*, *The Masks of Time*, *Downward to the Earth*, and *The Tower of Glass*.